Kenerly Presents Publications
P.O. Box 562674
Charlotte, NC 28213

kenerlypresents.com

shauntakenerlypresents@gmail.com

Charlotte, N.C.

ISBN-13: 978-0692668184
ISBN-10: 0692668187

First Edition: February 2016

10 9 8 7 6 5 4 3 2 1

Cover Design: AMB Branding

Printed in the United States of America

LOVE SLAVE

ANITRA HILL

ACKNOWLEDGMENTS

I first have to thank God for giving me such an amazing gift of writing! He has given me the strength and the guidance to keep going and to not give up on my dreams. To him I owe everything, he has been blessing me for 36 years now and has never given up on me. I am grateful for every opportunity that has been given, also thankful for every "No" when I wanted it to be a yes. He knew best and the opportunity was presented to me only when he said that it was right timing. I thank him for the favor that he has over my life!

I also want to thank my family and my friends that have always has constantly supported me and pushed me to never give up. (My parents, especially My Mom, Freakie Heavie yall, My Big Brother Matt, Kareen and Bryson, siblings, Ro, Ke, Pinky, Aunts and Uncles, cousins, Nieces and Nephews) I will NOT stop until I get to the top, I have too many people that's depending on me to be great. There are people that has believed in me since day 1. When I didn't even believe in myself, there were a few of you that always made sure that I knew that I had what it took. I want to name drop but I'm afraid that I will leave someone out, but please charge it to my mind and definitely not my heart.

The few that come to mind are:
*My beautiful God Sister, Nickey (Always did what it took to make sure that I was straight)
*My best friend Granny (One that gives me plenty to write about) "My Marsha Brady and I'm her Jane Brady"

3

*My Bestie Shamekia (The reason that I first got published, she's always claimed my greatness) *My Business Partner Takiya (From the gate she has showed love and pushed my work like no other simply because I was a hometown girl just trying to do my thing and make a name for myself) "MyHazel"

*⅔ of the 3 Amigos Author Nikki Rountree and Terrie L. Branch (Let's go! We working ova here and we're headed to the top!) -WeAreShe-

There are a host of others such as my first friend Lapina, Jr. Blount, Shell Road Crew
(especially Monique Robinson, Lady Boom, Big Ron and Elvis for always supporting) Terri Gambino, Angie, Susie and Mike, Ashley, Redd, The Porter's, Big Sis Cynt, My Snookie, My classy friend Tisha, Ray, Sharnel, Sissy Tierra, Sis Dree Jones, Chico, Natasha Knight #PGS baby, Showtyme, My Choc & Boo Brown, KiKi Swinson for first giving me a chance, LaJill Hunt, Candy and Lu, Britt and Candice (my most favorite sups in life), Rascoe, Melisa and Fat Mama, My City of Portsmouth Parking Authority crew, Will, Dara and Gank, Dad Darrell Wardlaw and the Thigpens, Rob Simmons of Simmons Bail Bonds, Dame and Kay, Keith Strother, EMo, Sweets, Shimmy and so many more that I'm sure that I can name. Just because your name isn't here please don't think that you're not appreciated. But please insert your name here
_____. Anyone that has ever read a novel, reshared a post, offered words of encouragement, I thank you!

Lastly but certainly not least... I want to thank The Realest Publisher on the planet... Thank you Shaunta Kenerly for believing in me and giving me the opportunity. You're one of my favorite people simply because you give so much of yourself to others, you give the most valuable thing that a person can ever have and that is KNOWLEDGE! You are simply amazing and I thank you for making me a part of Team Kinerly Presents. Writing is what I love to do, for it is my passion and a healing method and I'm thankful to be able to do what I love! I respect your hustle and can't help but to shine under you!

#PenGameStrong

Dear little black book…

She sat there with lust in her eyes as her bare breast were exposed. Nothing on but her fishnets and black thongs which were sitting dead in the crack of her honey suckled ass. My shiny handcuffs binding her wrist together. I have once again sucked her soul out of her body through her cream filled pussy until she begged me to stop. I then pulled out my crooked piece of steel from out of my boxer hole and allowed her to watch me as I stroked my dick for dear life. She began to moan. This was the moment that she begged me to let all of my semen splatter all over her flawless face for her nightly facial... She opened her mouth with the attempt to catch every single drop. And people wondered why I was so in love with this filthy fucking whore... Asia Monroe was my dirty little secret, my own personal love slave... (Until next time)

I allowed my pen to drop. I thought back over my session tonight with one of my sex angels. She became one of my sex slaves and I must say that I was quite impressed at myself with my performance.

Raven, which was my wife had given me this little black book so that I could keep my memorable moments in. Now at first I thought that this had to be some bitch ass shit. Me, Zavier keeping a fucking journal, (haahh) you have to be shitting me, but damn this thing might surely come in handy one of these days.

I had to admit that I did have a deep love for sex with women with clean, tight and wet ass gushy pussy! Me personally, I find it rather hard to turn down certain beautiful women with that wet wet. Matter of fact, there is nothing better than some 'loyal pussy' but some 'new loyal pussy!' I took pride in owning each piece of pussy that I fell up in more than once. I mean, I'm a man with a weakness and this weakness is hard to shake. (shakes head and then grins)

Chapter 1
Zavier "Speedy" Wright

Let me introduce myself, I'm 32 year old Zavier "Speedy" Wright and I'm a former professional Heavyweight boxer. Fighting was another passion of mines for 8 full years. I had a run full of challenging matches with some of the best of the best fighters from all over the world. Unfortunately, my career rapidly ended after a swift blow to the head by my opponent Joe Tobias. Joe was a great fighter but I should have won this match. Not trying to sound cocky or nothing, but ya boy was the shit! On this day my speed was much slower than normal and as soon as I was hit with the fourth blow to the head, that was all she wrote. I was out cold and that last blow was what ended my career and I hated it. I was knocked out by Joe but everyone that followed my fights knew that I wasn't at my best, so they knew that it wasn't necessarily the power of his punch. I had endured much more powerful punches then the one that had taken me out. The doctors had to make me realize that it was the repeated head blows that I had sustained that made my processing speeds slower and it also did major damage to certain brain functions. I can hear Dr. Batts in my head right now saying "Zavier repetitive head trauma could be a

greater risk factor for Alzheimer's disease and is also considered the main cause for CTE (Chronic Traumatic Encephalopathy) and is a well-known form of dementia. CTE is a progressive disease of the brain in which is linked to Memory loss, confusion, impaired judgment, aggression, depression and progressive dementia." This was when the studies, testing and research started. I had MRI scans to assess my brain and they discovered that my brain functionality was far more damaged than they thought.

My career was surely over and it seemed as if my whole life had ended, boxing was my everything and I couldn't imagine life without the love of my life. Along with sex boxing was my outlet from the world, my escape from reality. It was like besides my women, my boxing took all of the hurt, pain and stress away just from from the worries of everyday life. There was one person who had never left my side and that was my lady, Raven Riddick Wright. She had been down with me for the last 17 years of my life. I didn't always do her right, and I can't make any excuses for the reasons that I do the things that I do to her, but I can say that if no one loves me, this beauty does. Standing 5'5 and thick in the thighs, with the face and personality of a beauty queen, she kept the heads turning but she only had eyes for me. I myself, like a lot of niggas nowadays often took my lady for granted but prayed that she never left me.

Raven "Ray" is my rock and sadly to say it but I DON'T DESERVE HER! I have given her many reasons to leave but she will always find a million and one reasons to stay. She refuses to give up on me so I'm guessing that I can't be half bad in her eyes. Many women would have left me just on the strength of me no longer being "THAT NIGGA", but lucky to say she was down for me before any of this boxing shit. With my disease it seemed as if she loved me more, and all she wanted was for me to be happy with the rest of my life. She was willing to do whatever it took to make her man happy, she honestly had to be the best thing that had ever happened to me. At one time I wouldn't have ever admitted it but I needed Raven just as I needed the blood that flowed through my veins and I just hoped that she wouldn't ever get tired of me before I realized and worked on getting it together. A man's ego can be a bitch, and that bitch will have you fucked with no rubber! She was perfect in every way, she didn't miss any of my doctor's appointments and also made sure that I took care of myself the best that I could. The doctor's shared things with her that they didn't share with me about my condition, but only because they felt as if she was the one that needed to know what to look for and what to expect. It was as if she had to help me fight this thing and she wanted to protect me from this, I could feel my speed to be slower and my memory had started to fade away. She never judged me or got upset when i would lose or

forget things. Raven simply deserved the world and I needed to be the one to give it to her.

I had enough money stashed in my account for us to live comfortably off of and Raven also had a business of her own, she had a Publishing company. She was her own boss, baby girl did good for herself. She loved to write but also made writer's dreams become a reality. She loved to build people up while others took pleasure in tearing people down. Because she dabbled in her writing she would also express to that writing was good for the soul. She pushed me to simply write down my feelings when she started to see me sitting there in pity. I had began to waddle in my own sorrow and she felt as if something had to be done, and it had to be done quickly. I started to feel alone, even with her by my side. I felt miserable and didn't have a desire for life anymore. I felt robbed, robbed of my dreams and aspirations. I just felt like a complete failure and then the lady of my life made the unthinkable happen, she showed me the beauty of life once again.

Pulling up in her pearl white Range Rover with the plush butter leather seats, with my seat laid back as she allowed me to just kick back and relax. With my NY Yankee fitted cap sitting low enough to only view my slanted hazed eyes. As I sat further reclined in my seat I caught a glance over at my Queen and just took a moment to admire her true physical

beauty. My shorty was the sexiest in the game and her flaws made her stand out from the rest even more. This glance made me realize that I am the luckiest nigga alive to be blessed with a true rider. Shorty asked for so little and for that reason alone I then knew that I needed to bless her with everything. Being as if she asked me for nothing, it was my duty as her man to figure out the things to make her the happiest that she has ever been. With another pull of the haze, the skunky scent took me off into another land, known to some as LaLa.

My mind was so clouded but that didn't stop me from accepting the fact that I was craving her pussy juices on my Rosae' beard. I needed her to shoot her poison inside of my veins. Not caring about the danger of the other cars on the streets or being caught by Hamptons finest (police), because they were often on the prowl. I gave her the option of pulling over and parking or challenging her driving skills under pressure, but her look of confusion told me that she wasn't sure of how to answer. But she soon found out my motive and then understood my meaning.

Dear little black book…

With her thigh length boots and her famous brand pencil skirt on her curvy hips, I somehow managed to push her panties to the side with thoughts of exploring her playground. She knew that I loved playing in her box and this time was no different. With my fingers going in *and out of* her in a circular motion, fast and then slow and then from side to side, she couldn't take the pressure anymore. She thought with her better judgement and pulled over to the closest location in sight in which happened to be a funeral home parking lot. Not caring who might have seen, she threw the truck in park and then kicked her left boot up on the freshly cleaned dash to make herself more convenient for me to maneuver to. Looking into her glassed eyes I could see her desire for me, she wanted me inside of her wet canal. She wanted me inside of her right then and there but I had other plans for her.

After sucking her juices off of my glazed fingertips, I manhandled her to have her head up against the window and her back up against the door as her pussy sat there staring in my face as if i had owed it something. Well maybe i did, it was there ready to be Disrespected and I must say that I am the man for the job. I have been known to be a Disrespectful son of a bitch!

Sending my saliva shooting from my mouth to land dead into her pussy opening, I found fun in playing a game of slurping it back up right along with her clear substances that dared to escape from her pussy without my permission. I used my lizard length tongue and pussy eating lips to give my mouth all that it had been longing for... Her... no scratch that... My sweet pussy with her marinade juices... I played in her box with my tongue like an artist would play the strings of his guitar. The roll of my tongue throughout her pussy is what drove her pretty ass crazy.

Before I could reach for the emergency towel that we kept inside of the Mr. Nasty sex box in the backseat (had to be prepared for situations like these), she began squirting all over the place. I sucked as much of it that I could take in and kept up with the sucking of her clit and the inward and outward motion of my fingers inside of her pulsating tunnel of wonderfulness. She lost it as my fingers touched her g-spot, the moving upward motion and the tickling sensation was her breaking point. She began to jerk and squirt again and I could have sworn that her head had then started to spin around as she released all over herself, myself and also had let out that sweet honey glaze on those luxury butter seats. "YOU FUCKIN BASTARD!" She shouted in a disrespectful but sexy tone. "Just give me that

fuckin nut. Give daddy all of that sweet nectar cause I know you got some more for me. Stop being so fuckin stingy with that shit mama, give me all of my shit. I worked for this shit Ray, now fuckin cum for daddy." After I said that she did just that. I knew what she liked and knew how to bring that shit out of her.

While she was attempting to catch her breath and gain her composure she playfully slapped my freshly cut head and then used her freshly manicured nails to run along the grain of my waves. I rested my head on her lap still looking dead at her hairless sex box that was sitting there poking from between her thicker than life thighs.

She looked at me and smiled a kind of sneaky grin and said "Good game coach, thanks for keeping me in the game." Then put her hand out for our signature dap! Yeah I know, my girl was just that cool with her cool ass. Seeing her satisfied, made me satisfied. I wiped her pussy clean of her juices and then adjusted her clothes and then sat back in my seat without wiping her off of my face. She questioned if I was going to wipe her off of me and I simply told her "Nope. I want to taste you all day. Why not just lick my lips and have the pleasure of tasting and smelling you without having to place my lips or my fingers on

you Mrs. Wright." She just winked and told me "Keep on keeping it nasty for me, you lil nasty bastard." And I hit her with "Just keep on feeding your pussy monster, you lil nasty bitch." (until next time)

Chapter 2
"KEEP FIGHTING"

Pulling out of the funeral home parking lot we both noticed the video cameras in the parking lot and both just busted out laughing and gave each other dap. We laughed up until we pulled into the parking lot of the brick building with a sign that read "KEEP FIGHTING" in big bold red letters. Raven parked and took the keys out of the ignition and turned the truck off and turned to me and said "Come on baby, say hello to your new passion." I could feel the confusion written all over my face, and she came around and opened up my door to help me out since I was apparently lost in thought.

As we walked closer to the building I asked her what was this place. She then looked at me with the biggest and proudest grin on her face and told me "Welcome home baby. This is your new gym. You need this. This is your new journey back into your happiness." She handed me the keys and then turned to walk back towards the truck.

I walked into the building seeing all of the training equipment. The brand new punching bags hanging from the amazing designed ceilings and

pictures on the walls of famous boxers along with many shots from my many fights were also framed and blown up along the walls. At the entrance of the lobby was a wax figure of me with my whole boxing uniform on, from the head wrap that I wore all the way down to my custom made boxing shoes that I wore in my last fight. They even still had a splatter of blood on them from Joe's busted lip on them. I loved it. Every bit of it and couldn't hold back my tears any longer. I felt like I could breathe again. I had reason to live again. I always wanted to teach the sport once I mastered it. Especially to new and young upcoming talents.

Raven walked in with her CC famous brand printed business bag and also a brown box that she handed me to unwrap and open. I just couldn't believe it. How did she get all this past me? She demanded that I open up the box and then open up the folder that she had just pulled from out of her bag. I couldn't hold back the tears as I pulled out the shadow box that protected my very own personalized boxing gloves that she had dipped in gold, with my nickname and favorite saying engraved "SPEEDY" "KEEP FIGHTING." I had to take it all in as I looked around the place still with the folder in my hand. Was I dreaming?

"No, you're not dreaming," she said. "But I'm teaching you to dream with your eyes open. You may

have lost the ability to fight, but no husband of mine will ever give up on his fight at life."

For the first time in a long time I did something that I used to do often and that was drop down on my knees and I prayed and thanked God for this woman before me. She was my savior and I owed her my life. She kneeled down beside me and began to pray with me and we held hands and cried to the Lord above for our blessings. Once my last tear fell I leaned down, I kissed my beauty queen and then kissed the brand new gym floor and told myself to "KEEP FIGHTING."

Raven led me into the office area of the establishment where there was a gold plated name plate on the door and a gold plaque on the desk. Then she pulled out my black leather rolling desk office chair. She went around and pulled out her chair. She sat down and crossed her elongated legs as I licked my lips to let her know that at that moment I was tasting her. She winked her eye at me and said "Open your folder Mr. Wright," in her most professional tone. I just couldn't take my eyes off of her. This woman was amazing in every way. Without removing my eyes off of her, I opened the manila folder that contained my business license for KEEP FIGHTING Inc. that also included her name, the contract on the building and also a list of staff members that she had interviewed and hired for me. She had everything in line and in order for the

business to open up in another 8 days. There was nothing left to be done but for me to meet the staff and welcome them into the family. I will run my business like my family and do everything that I can to make sure that each one of my clients will become the best fighter that they can be. I will match their dedication times 10, to make sure that they get the best experience possible.

Dear little black book...

Walking over to my wife and picking her up and throwing her gently onto my cherry oak desk, she was about to find out about this beast that had been brewing inside of me all day. She laid on her perfectly slightly pudgy stomach. She seemed to be crying but with a naughty look plastered across her beautiful face. With her hair hanging in her eyes she says "Mr. Wright please don't hurt me, take it easy with me." Raven loved to role play and she definitely matched my nasty ways.

"I fuckin love you Ray, I don't think that you understand what exactly it is that you do to me. You must get all of this dick, so that I can make you understand what this shit means to me."

She peeked over her shoulder just in time to catch the first tear fall from my eyelids. My eyes were playing with my emotions. As soon as the third tear fell she wiped it from my cheek. I jammed my fingers inside of her to make sure that her sex box was ready for what she was about to experience. Before I could enter her raw she stopped me and did a move where she spinned around on the desk to where her head was now at my crotch. The heels of her thigh high boots were now in my desk chair and before I even knew it

she had my zipper undone. My curved dick in her hands ready to savor the taste of the blueprint of my babies but only if I would allowed her to. She licked her lips that were painted with my favorite shade of candy apple red lipstick. That let me know that it was getting ready to get real. She opened her mouth so wide that I could see her tonsils. Her throat expand and then she swallowed the shaft of my dick and all I felt was the wetness and the warmness of her throat. She sucked and sucked and slurped her saliva from off of my glossy thick and long rod that she seemed to play hide and go seek with. In and then out, stroking and then sucking, gripping and then moving down to my balls. Under my balls was the spot that made me spit out every curse word that has ever existed, like… "FUCK, SHIT, DAMNNNN, GAT DAMN IT BITCH, SHIIIIIIIIIT MUAFUCKA… DAMNNN BAE!" This was the place that she wanted me to be. Once she felt me reach my point of throbbing, she stopped sucking and then removed me from out of her mouth. Then she once again swung herself around on the desk and then managed to plant her feet on the floor and bent her pretty brown ass over the desk just waiting for me to enter her freaky ass from behind. She reached down and put her fingers where she wanted my rock hard manhood to go. She played with her pussy as I ran my thickness

of my dickhead along her opening in a teasing motion. She begged me to stroke her, but I loved to see her beg. She was guessing that I was taking too long to pleasure her so she took her finger out of her and put them in my mouth. Then Raven grabbed my dick and guided it to where she wanted it. Her tunnel had tightened right back up and was beyond moist. Stroking her slow only to pace myself made her scream my name. She reached behind herself and gripped my waist for me to give her more of me. Little by little I made her beg for more and then once I felt her flood gates open up. I fucked her like she had asked me too. I beat her pussy up and did as she asked me to and disrespected the fuck out of her safe haven. She had the skill of tightening her pussy muscles while I was in her fast to bring me to the point of exploding. She begged that I came with her and she came. I shot up all in her pussy walls with no remorse. Shit, I love my Bitch… Hands down, she held the title of 'My Own Personal Love Slave' in the flesh. No other female could ever compare. No matter what I tell these other hoes… (until next time) …

Pen drops

Chapter 3
Up and Running

The gym had been up and running and doing great for the last 3 months now. I had met some great clients. One in particular was teenager Ramone "Mone" Sykes. Ramone was a beast already and he had a passion for the game. I was in love with his drive and dedication. I often pictured my future unborn son to one day be the mirror of Mone. He was so eager to learn more and was always looking to better himself. He was fast as the speed of lightening. His family couldn't really afford to pay for his 3 day per week training classes, but they knew that he had the potential and could soon one day be the next big name boxer. Because I felt privileged and loved the passion in his eyes for the game, I allowed them to pay for the Wednesday classes and I threw in the Thursday and Friday classes for free. I just didn't want them to give up on his future.

Ramone trained hard and I pushed him to his limit and he never gave up on me. He was ready for a fight but I wanted to train him a little more. Then I would put him out there like his parents had asked me to.

I hadn't even realized that all of my staff had gone home for the night, so Ramone and I had been the only ones left there in the gym. The Friday night train session had now come to an end. Ramone got changed and then his father was there to pick him up. He gave me dap and left.

After he left out of the gym I came from the back of the gym to lock up when I'd noticed a pretty redbone patiently sitting in the lobby with her cheetah print upper thigh length dress on. Her thighs allowed my eyes to play peek a boo with that fat thing sitting between her legs. This honey was bad and even before we had exchanged any words I could tell that she wanted to fuck.

Looking at her for a second longer and then I decided to extend my hand out to her and greet her. She licked her lips and then stood up and said, "So you're the infamous Speedy Wright that my sister and my nephew has been talking so highly of huh? Well hello Speedy, just call me Joy. I just had to come and check out who my sister had been crushing on. My sister is afraid to go after what she likes but guess what Mr. Wright, I am not." She stepped a little closer to get a sniff of my neck and then placed her hand on my chest. I noticed the ring that stood out on her ring finger but that bothered neither of us.

"How can I be of service to you Joy?" I asked.

She paused and looked around. "You can start by giving me a tour of this amazing workplace that you have here sir."

I looked for a little bit longer and laughed in the inside because of the game that she tried to ran on me, as if I hadn't played these games before. She began to walk through the gym and I followed behind her and had the chance to admire her from head to toe from the back. She was draped in diamonds and she was also well put together. From the crown of her head in which was laid and not a single piece of hair out of place until it got down to the red bottoms on the soles of her feet. She was definitely a sight to see and she knew it. Once she got into the gym where the punching bags were located, she stopped and grinned, "Right here is where I want you Speedy." I looked at her in shock because she was definitely straight forward with hers and it was kind of turning me on.

"What's up, you down?" she asked, and I couldn't let her punk me like I was scared or something.

She walked towards the supply cabinet and seen the boxing gloves hanging on the outside. She removed her cheetah dress that hugged her perfectly sculpted frame and was down to her Secret's bra and panty thong set and red bottoms along with my

boxing gloves. She definitely knew how to get my attention. Joy had my big man's attention as well. Shorty had a perfect frame and a sexy ass disposition and I had to have my way with her...

Dear little black book...

Lord please forgive me for what I am about to do to this child of yours. But she is truly about to be my victim, my opponent and I must take her down in this ring... Ding! Ding! Ding!

She positioned me onto the mats and asked me to hold my hands up as she boxed with me with nothing but her panties and bra sitting perfectly on her lighter brown flawless skin. She took each piece of my clothing off with each punch that she took. Now down to nothing but my boxer shorts and socks. She admired my cut up body that I worked so hard to maintain. She rubbed her hands over each muscle and kissed my triceps as she licked her lips. She asked me to take a seat on the mats and then began to do things with her ass that I had only seen in the higher end strip clubs. I watched the show as she made rhythm with her ass cheeks and played with her D-cup breast at the same time. As I had gotten lost in her show before I knew it she had made her way over to me and straddled my lap right there on the mats. She had the boxing gloves now placed around her neck and started to gyrate her hips causing my dick to jump. She stopped and demanded me to listen to her and follow her instructions. I nodded like a little kid being

disciplined, waiting patiently. "Don't ever ask me my real name. It will always be Joy to you. And do not ask me personal questions. I will come to you, you will never come to me. There will be no kissing. Kissing is way too personal and lastly DO NOT ever think of falling in love or catching feelings. It's only sex between Joy and ummmm... I'll just call you Pablo! Yep, you will be my Pablo. Got it? Is this cool with you?" She asks.

I couldn't help but to smile because I love her take charge mentality. She reminded me so much of myself. Needless to say that I agreed and from there it was a wrap.

Laying there watching her was when she pulled out a gold package that contained our protection. She didn't even allow me to fill my dick of the condom. She did it all! With no head and no pussy eating or kissing, this broad did her thing. She rode my dick like it was going somewhere. The sit and spin move that she hit, all while tightening her vaginal muscles was unbelievable. Her pussy leaked her creamy substances as she knew each spot that she wanted to be hit. The more that I rammed my dick into each side of her walls from underneath her she moaned and refused to hold back her cum. It was as if the man that had placed that ring on her

wedding finger wasn't doing his job because the way that she came on me, it was as if she had been enjoying it all too much. Although it was none of my business, I wanted to know more. It was against the rules but this honey was doing something to me through her movement. She was sitting on a pot of gold and she knew it. As I grabbed her waist and pulled her down onto my stick, my dick thrusted inside of her hole. The faster I went the more she came and the more she came the faster I went. I wanted more and I was still in her, but I was thinking about the next time that I would bless her ovaries with my feel. I worked my hips in a circular motion so that I could swipe every avenue of her inner canal and that's when I got her to break.

"Cum with me daddy, pleaasseee cum with me Speedy," she said in a moan of pleasure.

I smiled because she was beginning to break her own rules. With a cocky grin on my face I had to acknowledge her weakness but of course after I let all of my nut empty out of my sack. "Ugh, that was amazing love but please stick to the rules that you set to play. I'm Pablo to you remember. No Speedy... That's way to personal."

She didn't seem to like being beat at her own game but I had to let her know who the man was.

She stood up and gave me a sly but cute little grin and put her clothes back on. Then she went and hung my gloves back where she had gotten them from. She blew me a kiss in the air and walked out of the gym like nothing had ever happened. Damn, that bitch was good with her shit. She will be back, I can guarantee that.

Another one under my belt... (until next time)

After cleaning up a bit at the gym and then locking up I returned home to my beautiful wife as if nothing had just happened. She appeared to be even more beautiful whenever I had done my dirt. My conscious didn't bother me because I had a way of blocking these things out and also my memory loss kind of helped a bit.

Raven was sitting at her home office desk with her eyes planted on her computer screen. I entered the doorway, she looked up and smiled an angelic smile and stood to greet me with a hug. She wore a sexy black lace floor length robe. She also had on a pair of heels with what seemed like to be the exact same bra and panty set that Joy had. I couldn't help

but smile at the thought of Joy but I had to admit that Raven was much more desirable and beautiful. She stood on her tip toes even in her heels and hugged my neck so tight. She asked how my day was as I kissed her forehead. I could smell the sweet smell that she often wore after her bubble baths. The smell of sweet honey kisses, mixed with her favorite body oil Amber White. It was such a great concoction together with her body chemistry and was sure to turn any man on.

I sat down on the couch that she had inside of her home office and she came and sat in my lap. I told her about my day in the gym. I couldn't help but to think of Joy my fresh and new 'love slave.' I dared not to mention Joy to Raven but that didn't stop her from crossing my mind. My thoughts must have gotten too deep into Joy because Raven felt my dick begin to poke her in her thigh. She smiled and told me that she knew that I wasn't thinking about feeling her insides at that time. I smiled and nodded but only because I couldn't tell her that I was thinking about somebody insides but they weren't hers. Just as she kissed me on my lips and stood to walk back towards her computer, she picked her cell phone up and started to scroll through it. Just then my cell phone began to vibrate. Looking at the screen, my mouth dropped as I read the message that came across the screen saying, "MY PABLO. CAN'T WAIT TO SEE YOU AGAIN." I couldn't help but to smile. Then I tried

to figure out how she got my number. What happened to the rule don't get too personal? Then I got nervous because Raven stood there at her desk with the same smile that I had on my face on hers. What did she know? Maybe even who had her smiling like Joy had me smiling should have been more of the question? The smile that I had on my face had just faded away at the thought of someone entertaining my lady the way that only that I should. Nahhhh... I trust my baby!!! I'm probably just tripping because I knew the things that I've been doing.

Chapter 4
A Turn For The Worse

Early morning doctor's appointments were the worse for me because I hated to get up and they always were full of bad news. I wasn't for it today. I refused to get up and I told Raven that I wasn't going. She said she was going without me. I turned back over and went back to sleep as she got up and got dressed. I should have been ashamed of myself for letting her go to my appointment with me even caring enough to care, but I'm tired of the bad news. I can feel myself getting more worse off. I'm just not into any more bad news. Just let me die happy.

After tossing and turning another 30 minutes after Raven left out of the door, I decided to get up and get showered and dressed. I decided to go and pick Ramone' up to take him to breakfast, just to thank him for all of his hard work he has been giving me during training. I called his mother's cell phone and asked her if it was ok to come and get him a little early for his training session and she agreed. His mother was happy that Ramone had another male figure in his life because his father didn't have all of the time in the world that Ramone deserved.

Ramone was a good kid and like me, boxing was his outlet. Today's life is so much harder for the kids nowadays. They had so much peer pressure to deal with. I enjoyed having Ramone around. He looked up to me and I lived through him. We needed one another and we were a perfect fit in one another's lives.

Pulling up to the gas station to fill up my brand new toy that I just purchased for myself. I bought a Pepsi blue Audi (4 rings is what I liked to call them) and I loved it. It was just what I needed to spice up my look, because with the dementia setting in I have started to look older and I felt older as well. My new baby made me feel better about myself. Hitting the skunky stuff a few more times and then turning my fitted to the back, I look at myself in the mirror and looked straight into my soul.

While sitting there as the herbs burned looking at myself, I thought over my life and realized that so many things had been taken from me. Material things had been taken from me but then again I had to say that all that God has taken, though he has given me so much more in return.

It was Santana Renee. She was my little church freak that I was trying to let go of. She refused to take NO for an answer. She went on and on as I purposely zoned out on her…

Dear little black book…

As I laid my head back on my head rest, she
kept asking questions as if I was answering any of
them. I let her talk because none of it was heard
until I heard her say "Well let me just suck your
dick one last time and then I'll let you go on about
your business." Before she could get the rest of
her sentence out, I had my dick standing at
attention outside of my boxer hole. She took no
time with swallowing it whole while I sat there
with my eyes closed as she got what the hell she
wanted from me. Santana Renee was my little
freaky bitch.

She hardly ever wanted any dick. She got
off by watching me get off. She knew how to
swallow a dick whole with no gag reflex and for
that she had her way with me. Who was I to stop
her from sucking me off? She had to have been
the real 'Superhead' because she knew just what
to do while my dick was in her mouth. She would
normally tie my hands together so that I wouldn't
try to play in her pussy while she sucked me off.

Today was a little different probably
because of the location, but in reality she didn't
really give a fuck. Something was different about
her. She didn't have the same desire in her eye's

for me. "FUCK IT," I thought. Let me just get this nut so her holier than thou ass can keep her ass truckin. My dick head touched the back of her throat and I could hear her making a humming noise and was massaging my balls. That shit drove me insane. I let it all loose in her mouth. She loved drinking my semen and I didn't stop her. Once she swallowed all of me and my body finally stopped shaking, she wiped her mouth and stood up and looked back at me and winked and was gone about her holy way.

I needed that "Just Because' head, without having to do anything for it. She was definitely my little church freak. One of the nastiest on the roster for sure. Good looking out on the head Sister Santana, see you at Sunday's church service, with your little nasty ass... Laughing out Loud (until next time)

Holding the black book as if it was my bible...

While sitting in my car at the pump while watching Santana walk away. She turned and gave me an awkward look and it sent chills up my spine because something was just different about this look. Before I could even pull the door knob to get out to go and pay for my gas, a guy with a ski mask on ran up on me with a pistol in hand and told me to give him

everything. My watch, ring, wallet, cell phone and car keys. Before I could make a move to give him anything there was a loud commotion coming from behind me. Afraid to look in my rearview mirror because of what the gunman might do, with another long blow of the horn the gunman ran away towards the rear of the store. Finally, able to take my eyes off of the young punk ass nigga that tried to get me for my shit. I finally was able to look behind me to see who had just possibly saved my life and the car was gone. No one was any longer there. How did they get away that fast? I'm confused. They were just there and blowing the horn repeatedly but now no one is there… Looking all around me to check my surroundings and once I saw that the coast was clear, I decided to say FUCK THAT GAS and sped off to clear myself of this scenery. I didn't know where the gunman had gotten off to and didn't know his motive and if he would try to come back for me, so I decided against staying there any longer.

Speeding into oncoming traffic without even noticing the distance of the cars coming my way was a dangerous move on my part. Tires screeching and squealing was all that was heard and then there was a LOUD BOOOOOOOOOOOM! With my head hitting the steering wheel and then feeling the car flipping several times. I couldn't move and I could feel my neck starting to let off a horrifying pain. I could hear several people yelling out "CALL AN AMBULANCE!

Sir are you okay? We're getting help for you!" There were cries and people screaming and hollering and then the ringing of sirens coming in my direction. Then everything seemed to go cloudy. I was fading and could hear my mother talking to me, she had been dead for 3 years now so how can I hear her tell me "Get your life together son. God kept you here for a purpose. You're a Wright son and your better than this." Fading out and then seeing a white light was all that I could remember…

3 days later

Opening my eyes felt like a task. They were so heavy. While trying to get them completely opened and able to focus on my surroundings was when I realized that I was no longer in my new whip or in my 5 bedroom home that we had built from the ground up. Yet I was in what seemed to be a hospital room. It was stuffy and there was an old school television hanging on the wall. Where's the flatscreen? Where's my cool blowing air conditioner? What has happened to me? It seems as if I had been set back a good 20 years. Everything was antique looking. Not my modern day looking things. I then started to realized how I had taken the finer things that I had acquired in my life for granted. That was when I heard a loud beep come from above my right shoulder, but wait I can't move to even look and see what the noise was. This had to be something awful that was happening to

me. "Think Speedy think. What was the last thing that you remember? I was going to pick Ramone up, but I don't remember anything after that. Wait, Santana Renee was the last person that I remember seeing. Was Ramone with me, asking myself as if I'm really trying to figure it all out in my head that had now began to throb uncontrollably.

I could hear a door squeaking as it sounded as if it was opening slowly. Footsteps were heard and then I heard a female's voice say "Mr. Wright, I'm so glad that you finally decided to come back to consciousness. We have been waiting on you." She then began to rub my temples as if she knew that it was relieving to my head. She left my head and then went to my chest and acted as if she was checking for a heartbeat. Once she left that area she went further down. She rubbed and then caressed. I could feel now, where at first it was if I had been paralyzed. She was stimulating me and my dick had begun to get rock hard and that was when she told me to just relax because I seemed to be tense. So, relax was what I decided to do for her.

Dear little black book…

I was really confused now, as I got a glance at this fine ass woman. She smelled like the dew on a melon. I could feel her unsnap something and then I felt the restraint from my neck unloosen. Finally, I could see this sex goddess. She was dressed in a short nursing dress in the angelic color of white. She let her breasts bulge out of her bra and these bitches are beautiful. It was as if she was reading my mind because she climbed on top of me and put her melons into my mouth. She felt like silk on my skin and tasted like honey in my mouth. She looked me dead in my eyes and it was as if she was looking dead into my soul. She placed her soft yet wet lips onto mine and ran her tongue across my lips in a teasing motion. Her tongue was her weapon and once she slid it into my mouth it was as if she had just pulled the trigger. POW… The motions that her gun was making in my mouth was unbelievable. She flickered and flipped it and teased me some more. Once she got tired of teasing the inside of my mouth she moved onto my neck and then my ear. She sucked and bit and licked on me and it was as if I could do nothing to stop her. Not that I wanted to but she had me in a trance. I wanted more but then again I needed her to stop. I needed to gain control but I couldn't.

She sucked my neck like she was a leach and no matter how much it hurt, it felt so good. She ripped my hospital gown open and ran her tongue down the center of my chest, not forgetting to pleasure my nipples. She drove me crazy! She knew exactly what I liked. She used her tongue like a ninja in a sword fight. She was no stranger to what she was doing. She got down to my navel and made a circular motion and then flipped herself so that her ass was looking dead in my face. Her dress was so skimpy that I could see her bare ass cheeks. No panties at all, all you saw was her plumped up ass cheeks and that pretty ass pussy of hers poking out.

With the jumping of her ass cheeks in my face, the sight made my mouth water up. She kissed the tip of my dick head and that was it! I went face first into her wetness and went deep sea diving and ate all that she had to offer without second thought. I was all up in that pussy while she sucked the life out of my dick but then doing CPR on it at the same time. While fucking her with my tongue from the back and fingering her pussy at the same time, she let her juices go all over my face. Her cum tasted like pineapples and strawberries. I slurped up everything that came out of her. The more that I slurped, the harder she sucked. The harder that she sucked, made me

42

want to fuck her so badly. Her pussy was throbbing in my mouth and I showed it no mercy. I wanted all of her juices. I didn't want to leave her any fluids. I wanted them all and I wasn't going to stop until she had nothing left. Nurse naughty was good at what she was doing and she knew it. The biting of her ass cheeks made her moan so loud and then all of a sudden she jumped up from my embrace. She hopped quickly on my dick and rode me in reverse like she hadn't had any dick inside of her in ages. She flexed her pussy muscles and rolled her hips so that I could feel every angle of her walls. Her insides felt like heaven. Wait, I'm in this bitch bare with no rubber so I really felt all of her. I'm tripping… I'm not supposed to be in her bare backed. I don't even know shorty. She bounced and played with her titties as she was pleasuring herself. Grabbing her hips and then pulling her hair from the back was when I started ramming my dick inside of her from beneath her. She threw her head back and her dreads hung freely and it was a beautiful vision in front of me. I went ham inside of her box of heaven. She enjoyed it. Every bit of it and so did I. She gripped my thighs and lifted her ass cheeks up off of me slightly and then spun around on me without taking my dick out of her. She fucked me as she looked into my eyes. It was sexy as hell, this passion that she fucked me with. It was as if

we had been here before. She had an exotic look about her. I had to concentrate hard so that I wouldn't bust too quick but being in this pussy raw had me on cloud nine. It was when she began to talk in some kind of Jamaican accent that took the cake for me. That shit was sexy as shit to me, she had no clue that she was driving me insane.

"Busss in me pusssssse rude boi," she said in a tone of authority.

I should have been pulling out of that tight and wet pussy. I added my liquids and painted her insides with my semen. What the hell was I thinking? Too late now, all I could do was pray that she didn't have nothing or that she doesn't get pregnant. But what's done is already done.

Like a professional, she pulled her dress down and straightened herself up and then winked her eye and walking out of the room as if nothing had just happened. No name or nothing.

Just like that nurse naughty was now just a memory. (until next time)

Laying there smiling and wondering how long I had been in this hospital bed and how I got to be so lucky. Even though I was in this hospital bed I still had

the pleasure of running up in that sexy ass Jamaican nurse. Gotta love that random pussy as well! Now it's time to get out of here and get back to work. I have to get Ramone in that ring for his first fight.

Thinking of Ramone and his career made me excited. Almost as excited as that Jamaican just made me. I found myself laughing to myself until the door crept open once again.

Walking into the room was my beautiful wife and a doctor. I was happy to see my baby until I realized that I hadn't washed 'Nurse Naughty' off of me. I hope that Raven don't get too close but knowing her she will. What was I thinking my wife hasn't seen me with my eyes open yet, so she will be all over me. They both turned their attention to me and both spoke and then continued on with their conversation.

An Asian nurse entered the room and came to my bedside and asked me how I was feeling and then continued to take my vital signs. I asked her if I was able to go to the bathroom. She then turned to the black male doctor that was in conversation with Raven to ask. The doctor felt that it was too risky for me to try to get up before I had another cat scan, so I settled for a warm rag to wipe my face with.

After washing my face, she then bought me a toothbrush and toothpaste and a portable bucket to

spit out my fluids. It was as if she smelled nurse naughty on my breath. As long as the one woman that I loved didn't care what the nurse thought. Raven paid me no mind. She was too indulged in a conversation with this black man. There was no telling what they had been talking about but I was trying to trust Raven, not every man was like me. Besides I knew that I had a great wife and these thoughts should never cross my mind. I had to think back on half of the encounters that I had with these random and meaningless ladies and then realized that if Raven had ever cheated on me, I deserved it.

Walking to the bed was the two of them. The doctor and Raven. The first to speak was Raven by kissing me on my lips as if she missed me. Asking her before she could say anything, "What happened to me baby"? She looked once again at the doctor and he then started his spill.

"Well Mr. Wright, I was just telling your wife about how lucky of a man that you are. You were involved in a three car accident and I don't know how you made it out, but you did! You were coming out of a gas station and you were hit by three different cars coming from different directions. Your car is totaled, but those are material things and your life is far more valuable. You have been in a coma for the last three days now. You didn't have a seat belt on and your head hit the steering wheel and the hit knocked you

unconscious. Your lovely wife was just telling me about your head injury due to boxing as well, so that threw up some red flags for me. What I want to do is send you for more testing to make sure that we didn't disrupt anything else inside of there."

By this time Raven was at my beside rubbing my hand as she knew that this would calm me. Anytime someone talked about my head injury I would become upset with the world. This little petty shit had fucked up my whole life and everything that I have ever worked for. Where I would normally tell this nigga where he could shove his opinion, my wife was my peace. Agreeing to his testing and just hopeful for a successful future with managing Ramone were the thoughts that I was now looking forward to.

After getting the test results back I learned that my injuries had worsened but I refused to let that stop me from living my life. Raven was stressing because she was afraid of losing me. I explained to her that God makes no mistakes. I had to be strong for her, even though on the inside it was killing me that my life could be taken at the blink of an eye. I had to display strength because that's the only way that I could convince Raven to be strong for me. I lived through her, in reality all of this time she had been my strength. My lady was amazing and I knew it. From that day on I held my head high and decided that I would live everyday as if it was my last.

After a full seven days in the hospital, it was now time to be released. I hadn't seen 'Nurse Naughty' anymore. I started to question if she had been real. I started to second guess myself with a lot of things now and wonder if it was because of my head injury that I was thinking that these things were happening. My whole life was becoming a blur right there in front of me but I'm determined to make it through.

Chapter 5
A Better Man

After being released from the hospital I was learning to become a better man. The biggest lesson that I learned during my hospital visit was to stop taking life for granted. Even though I had just crashed my baby, I went and copped another one and in the same color of Pepsi Blue. I had to learn to humble myself again. I lost it somewhere along the way. These material things could be taken away in the blink of an eye so I had to learn how to appreciate the simple things in life once again.

In my search of finding myself once again, I fell in love with giving rather than receiving and I must say that it felt good. Beginning with Ramone, I no longer charged his family for his training sessions. They were honest hard working people and just wanted to see their son make something of himself. Ramone really looked up to me so I had to give him an example to be like. The more energy that I put into him the more I seen the beauty of his love for the sport start to excel. I was determined to make something of him, simply because he was hungry for it. He wanted it, he wasn't like the average young cat.

He would rather train with me then hang out in the street.

Watching him in his butterfly stage made me proud, so I decided to give him something that he would always remember. I took him to Las Vegas to see a main event big name fight. I had never been to a Mike Tiller fight but It would be our first experience together. He was a good kid and deserved that plus more. We stayed in Vegas for 2 days and he had the time of his life. It was beautiful seeing other people happy. It made me happy to see them happy.

On the last day of us being in Vegas, I decided that we would do something different. We got dressed up and went to one of the finest restaurants/lounges that was hosting a R&B concert with a few old school artists along with new school singers as well. He was a different kid. Where most teenagers only listened to rap he was the opposite. He liked rap but he also loved some oldie but goodies. That was mostly what I played in the gym and also his grandmother had a big influence on his life. He was being raised right and it gave me pleasure to be so close to him.

The after lounge was packed and Ramone was one of the youngest in the spot but he blended right in. He found his way around the establishment and found a young lady that was a few years older than him.

They chopped it up for most of the night. While he did his thing I scoped the room. Things were different for me. All the women in there were different but all looked the same in my eyes. It seemed as if no one stood alone, but had the same agendas. While vibing to the music, I decided to text my wife and let her know that I was thinking of her. She hit me with a quick reply back and told me that she was just thinking about me and wanted to feel me inside of her. She knew that this shit excited me. I love the nasty side of this queen. She knew exactly what she was doing and it made my dick bulge in my pants. As I waited for her next nasty reply I could feel someone staring at me. Fixing my dick in my boxers through my pants I tried to check out the scene to see who it was that was staring a hole into my sole.

She was beautiful. She looked a lot like a little Indian doll. She stared with a seductive look on her face that let me know that she saw something that she liked. While she caught me with my hand on my dick, she smiled and licked her lips. Trying to not look too pressed. I checked my phone for Raven's response and she hadn't said anything back yet. Looking back over in the direction of the Indian doll, I noticed that she was gone. Looking around the lounge was useless because there were so many people in there that it was impossible to spot her. Ramone had came over and asked was I ok and then headed back over to the little model type of chick with

a grin plastered across his face. He was living the life, not yet 18 and in a grown and sexy lounge. He looked every bit of 25 and acted like he was about that age as well.

While vibing to the music I felt my phone vibrate and when I reached for it was when I spotted India (that's the name I'll give her for now). She stood there by herself but confident in her skin. She stood about 5'5, about 185 and as thick as a brick. Her skin was the color of cocoa, but you could tell that she was a thoroughbred. She stood with so much cool about her, she didn't need a group of girls around her to make her feel powerful. She had a baby face so I could tell that she was a little younger. Feeling my phone vibrate once again I reached into my pocket but this time without taking my eyes off of my prey. She blushed and then pulled out her cell phone and pretended to look interested at what info it contained. Seeing that it was Raven calling I walked towards the pretty lady, all while answering my phone. I stepped right in front of her to be sure that she would not get away from me again. After listening to Raven tell me how much she misses me and can't wait for me to get up in her guts, I advised her that I would be home early the next day and told her to keep it wet and tight for me and I'll take care of it. Raven sighed in my ear so I could tell that she wasn't too happy that I didn't have too much conversation for her right then but I would make it up to her when I got to the crib. After

telling her that I would call her before bed, she smacked her lips and then disconnected. I made a mental note to pick her out a I'm Sorry gift but right now I have work to do. That work was to figure out this young lady's story.

"Hey love, I'm Zavier and may I ask you your name?" Zavier said in a smooth tone.

She smiled and showed her flirty side by replying "I know who you are Mr. Speedy Wright. I'm a big fan of yours. I used to follow your fights, thanks to my father! He was a very big boxing fan and he got me into following the sport and you just so happen to have been one of my favorite fighters. I remember having the biggest crush on you and told my parents that I was going to meet you one of these days and look at this… Here you are in the flesh!"

I couldn't help but to be a bit flattered, I thought that I was admiring her and she was a fan of mines. After standing there and talking to her for the next 45 minutes, I learned that she was 25 year old Armani Bridges from Baltimore, Maryland. She snapped pictures of the two of us and told me that she would always tell her father that she would one day marry me! We both laughed and then made more small talk. She was a great young lady and loved older men, but I then knew that I couldn't ruin her life like I would do if I was to start anything with her.

We shared a couple rounds of drinks and played a couple of games of pool as we learned more about one another. Talking to her made me realize that I had damaged a lot of souls and I refused to do that to her. She was very intrigued by me and seemed to enjoy getting to know me on a personal level. Where a lot of women were only interested in what they could get out of the deal, she was different. Armani genuinely wanted to know me. She sat and listened to every detail that I shared with her about my life. She was a good girl and she deserved to be happy. I prayed that the Lord sent happiness her way because she deserved it.

Ramone came over and told me that him and his little female friend would be going out to see the city together and he asked me if it was ok with it. I was kind of hesitant at first but I realized that I had to let him grow up. I told him to be back by 1 a.m. and to keep his phone by his side, he agreed and then they were out. I guess it would be Armani and I until she was ready to go in for the night.

We spent the remainder of the night walking and talking and drinking. She was great company and I loved her conversation. Many females these days didn't have any conversation, if it wasn't about sex or your money they couldn't hold a decent convo. But Armani was different. She was a great young lady. If I would have met her before I met Raven then she may

of stood a chance. She reminded me a lot of Raven though, she was a true go-getter. She was cool as a fan and filled with class, she wasn't the ghetto type. I really liked her and wanted us to surely keep in contact with one another. We walked on the strip and enjoyed the views while the passer byers looking at us as if we were a couple. We both laughed as a few people stopped and told us that we made a cute couple as we snapped pictures together. We never corrected them, we just smiled and kept it moving.

I could see the lust in her eyes for me and I have to admit that I felt something for her as well but the truth of the matter was that I loved my wife. She didn't deserve the things that I have done to her over the years. Looking at Armani was as if I was looking into the soul of Raven all over again, back when we started loving one another. She had an innocence about her and all she wanted was to be loved right. I could tell that she was falling for me by the way that she looked at me. She just gazed into my eyes as I talked. She appreciated my time as I did hers. I was wishing that I could remove the hurt from her heart.

Listening to her stories about the men that she has given herself to were no better than me and I hated it. For her to have been such a young lady, she has experienced a whole lot in her years. She told me stories about her grandfather molesting her time and time again. She was broken. Many men have taken

her for granted over the years and all she has ever did was look for love. Although she searched in all the wrong places, she still deserved to be treated like the young queen that she is. I find it sad when women knew their worth but didn't demand what they deserved. They would settle for less just to feel the love of somebody, or what seemed to have copied the actions of love.

As I sat and listened to her stories, I saw myself and my engagements with all of these women over the years. I never led them on in my opinion, but I knew that I had no intentions on being with them either. It was just sex with me. I loved sex! I loved watching these women fall to their knees for me to become my very own love slave.

I had the power to have almost any woman that I wanted. Not trying to say that I was a God or nothing but it was just something that they loved about me. I was blessed I like to think, the opposite sex just flocked to me. It was never my intentions to make anyone feel any type of hurt behind me, but to get that bit of satisfaction for that moment. I loved the opposite sex. They were simply beautiful and worthy of being pleased. They all deserved to feel loved and I wanted to do my part, one woman at a time.

The way that Armani swung her hair and the sway of her hips as she walked in front of me made

me want to take back all that I had just said about not wanting to destroy her. She wanted me inside of her and Lord knows I needed to be there as well. I was fighting with myself trying not to do her as I have done every other woman that I came across.

She wanted it but I had to be strong about this one. It was something about her, she kept my attention. She was fine as hell and she knew it, but she didn't use it the way that she could have. She respected me the way that I respected her and the flames were mutual for one another. I had to shake this feeling because I felt myself getting weaker for her by the moment. We walked further and further through Sin City while trying not to sin, but temptation was winning the arm wrestling battle. Neither of us wanted to speak on the obvious sexual attraction for one another but the heat was getting hotter.

She walked inside of the Flamingo Hotel and led me towards the casino. She grabbed a drink from off of the cocktail tray. She headed towards the quarter slot machines and sat at a machine and I followed suite and sat at the machine beside her. She looked over at me and winked her eyes and then inserted a quarter into the machine. Pulling the handle and then blowing a kiss in my direction as she watched the wheels of the machine spin.

1 cherry… 2 cherries… 3 cherries… Ding! Ding! Ding!

We have a winner flashed across the machine! One quarter made her a thousand dollars, just that quick. She must have had a lucky streak going on. She put another quarter into my machine as she waited for them to come to her machine to claim her winnings. She kissed me on the lips and then pulled the lever once again and just like that, she had the machines in a trance. This one was going off as well, she hit another match just off of two quarters. As we sat there and waited on them so that she could claim her money, she sat on my lap as she waited. She grabbed another cocktail off of the tray of the show girl that was walking past and guzzled it. Before the young lady could walk away, she grabbed another one and by then she was done. She started to feel a little more tipsier than before because she was now in my lap and gyrating her hips on my dick. She moved as if she heard music in her head and as she moved my dick felt her movement. My guy began to rise to the occasion. I tried to ignore her but my dick had other things in mind.

After claiming her winnings of five thousand dollars and inserting only two quarters and four cocktails later I was helping her walk out of there. She wasn't feeling any pain and she took every opportunity to hold onto me and get her feel on as

well. I asked her where she was staying and she told me that she was staying there at the Flamingo and reached into her name brand designer bag and retrieved her keycard that had the numbers 2801 PH on it. She was on the penthouse floor. Shorty had some bread. She looked at me sadly as we waited on the elevator. Just that quick it was as if a bit of sadness had come over her. Once the elevator opened and we walked in, there was no one there to separate us. She was all over me, all that built up friction that I saw in her eyes earlier came to the light. She turned to face me and looked me dead in my eyes and told me "Please just take me, just this one time."

I looked at her puzzled like, waiting to see what was to come out of her mouth next. "See Speedy, the doctor gave me a few months more to live due to my cancer diagnosis. I just want to leave this place happily. I know that you're married and I want to respect that but I can't deny my attraction to you. You have made tonight one of the happiest nights of my life and I thank you for that. You have been the perfect gentleman and I thank you. I don't want this perfect night to end."

Without hesitating she grabbed my head and kissed me so sensually. She caught me by surprise but I couldn't deny her invite. I tried to gather what bomb that she had just dropped on me. I now

understood her sadness. Just then her tongue danced in my mouth and got tangled up with mine. She knew how to use her tongue and she was beginning to get me wrapped up in her web. The place that I was trying to escape she was pulling me into. I wasn't trying to get pulled into her sexual web but she was testing me and I was failing badly. Temptation was a mutha fucka. I didn't want to give her the business but she was asking for it! Who was I to not respect her last wishes? She deserved to go out happily. I must admit that her bad news brought about a bit of sadness in me as well, but I was determined to make sure that she didn't have any sad moments while with me.

Dear little black book…

    The ride up to the Penthouse floor was a very spicy one. Her dress decided to make its way up her voluptuous thighs, exposing her everything. She was sexy as hell and I could not deny that everything in me was wanting to fuck the shit out of her. She ran her tongue along the rim of my ear and whispered in my ear "I will have my way with you, stop trying to fight it." That was it, she just told me that she would not take NO for an answer. She ran her fingers across the print of my pants and then went down to her knees and put her mouth on the bulge in my pants. Even through my pants her tongue did a number on my dick. She played with my balls and lightly bite at my shaft. I pulled her back up and just looked at her. I ran my fingers through her shoulder length dreaded hair and traced her features with my finger tips and she loved it. She laid her head on my chest and then began to play with my nipples through my shirt. The funny thing was that I have never really had a thing for my nipples being played with but this honey had me going.

    The elevator door opened slowly but this didn't stop Armani. She wasn't ashamed to let the world see that she was ready for what she was about to do. The bellboy glanced at me and gave

me a slight grin. I had a small look of embarrassment on my face, but she didn't care. He got off on the next floor and once he exited the ride she watched herself in the mirror behind her and this seemed to excite her even more. She jumped into my arms and watched as she slung her hair back and then continued to tease the shit out of me. Finally reaching the 28th floor was when the games began. She pulled out her cellphone and began to snap more pictures of the two of us. She did all types of seductive poses on me, all while grabbing my penis. She kissed on me, wrapping my hands around her waist and also unbuttoned her blouse while placing my hands on her DD size cups. As we reached the door, I fumbled with the room key. What has always seemed to be the easiest thing to do was now seeming to be the most difficult. I couldn't get the key into the hole, she had me so distracted that I couldn't focus. Finally getting the keycard into the slot I now had the problem of making the key entry indicator light to turn green. It kept flashing red and at this time I'm guessing I was taking to long for her liking because she turned and grabbed the key out of my hand and slid it in slowly and it finally turned green. It was like walking into a new world inside of the suite. In a flash she was down to nothing but her stilettos, tattoos and nothing else at all. As she turned to

face me, my phone began to vibrate and it was Ramone. I had to answer it, I needed to know if he was ok. She watched as I hit the answer button and then took advantage of the opportunity. As I was listening to Ramone talk about his night, she began to undress me. Starting with my Lo shirt and wife beater, she then licked my nipples in a circular motion. This drove chills up my spine and then she worked her way down to my belt, and then next my pants. As she exposed my boxer briefs, she pulled my dick out of its bondage (my boxer briefs). Her face lit up as she witnessed all 10 inches of my greased up dick sitting there staring at her saluting.

Hearing nothing of what Ramone was saying, I hung up the phone as he said "Ok Pop's I'll holla at you when you get here." I threw my phone across the room once she started to kiss on my bare skin. She smelled like my favorite scent on a female, I knew it from anywhere. The scent of Very Sexy filled my nose and this made me even harder. She stroked my dick all while running her thumb across its head in a circular motion. As she did this my clear substances began to leak from out of its hiding place. She licked my precum and smiled as if she was pleased with its taste. I had to admit that I am a sucker for some good head and with the way that

she was man handling my dick head. I couldn't wait for her to take all of me in. I ran my fingertips across her body, she moved in a sensual way that let me know that my touch was making her warm. Once I got to her neck, I played with her neckline and then the small of her back and she arched that mutha fucka like she was ready for me to enter. Her arch was perfect, I could vision entering her from behind and watching her ass cheeks clap to its own beat. I then guided her head back to my dick to let her know that I was ready for some head. Licking my balls came first and then she opened her mouth so wide that she swallowed my dick whole before I even knew it. I grabbed her neck once again to control her intake and outtake. She definitely knew what the fuck she was doing and she had me on edge. Putting her head down further, she not only licked my balls but she also licked this certain spot right under my balls that drove me crazy. She was unusually close to my ass, I wasn't sure if I was supposed to enjoy it this much. Her tongue sent a bolt shooting through me. I was enjoying her a little too much, she wanted to do all of the pleasing. I felt helpless, she had me weak in the knees. I couldn't let her get the best of me without giving her a little tongue action. Flipping her onto her side, I handled her. She was about to get this work and she didn't even know it. Slightly biting

her thighs and kissing at the same time, she tried to squirm with each feel of my tongue. Pulling her back to me was when I found her knees unlock the keys to the private safe. Her knees were a tender spot for her. Running my tongue over her left knee drove her crazily insane. She didn't even know what this spot was doing to her but with the release of her cum that oozed from her pussy, told me a secret that she never knew that she had.

After about three nuts later was when I started to lick her pussy and suck her juices. It was as if I had just unlocked a new level of nasty on her. She moaned louder and louder as my pussy eating skills amazed her and gave her pleasure all at the same time. Finding her asshole as it invited my tongue to lick its avenues as well. The harder she fucked my face the deeper I went. "Give me dick," she screamed and that I was going to do. Sucking her soul through my imaginary straw made her cream all over my face. Once she came once more was when I pulled the gold pack from the nightstand. I slid it onto my throbbing dick, asked her how she wanted it first. She climbed onto all four and said in the most sexiest tone "From the back Speedy, I like it from the back." Taking a second out to view her from that angle, made me realize that she had the body of a goddess. She whined because she was ready

to be fucked. Running the head of my dick along the opening of her pussy made her move to follow my lead. She was ready for it, but I continued to tease. I finally made my way inside of her, instead of soft and slow I rammed my dick in her. She liked it rough, I could tell. She hollered out and I threw it back in there in the same motion as before. She liked it and I slapped her ass and pulled it out and watched her beg for more. Fucking her and watching her head bang the headboard at the same time. She cried out for more and asked "Why are you fucking me like this Speedy?" I asked her if she wanted me to stop. She replied "You better not, fuck me. FUCK ME NOW!" Grabbing her shoulders and pulling her into me and allowing my dick to play inside of her guts. She was beginning to look as if she was possessed. Her eyes rolled to the back of her head and her mouth hung open. She looked as if she needed to catch her breath so I removed myself from out of her and she smacked her lips as if she was upset. I went and grabbed her a bottle of water from out of the fridge and got a bottle for myself as well. Once I climbed back into the bed she attacked me. She straddled my lap and without anything extra being done, my dick stood right back up. She filled her pussy with my hardened rod and teased me slowly. While straddling me she planted both of her feet on the

bed as if she was standing up slightly and doing squats while she then watched my dick enter into her while on her feet. She was winding slow and moved her hips in a gyrating motion as my dick hit every angle of her walls. Her pussy was tight as fuck and it felt good as a virgin. She placed my hands on her soft breasts and demanded that I play with her titties and grip them to guide her frame down onto mine. She knew just how to use her pussy muscles to tighten and grip her lips onto my shaft. Once she came on my dick once more, she lost a lot of energy from coming so hard. I then decided to take back over.

As I sat in the chair that sat at the bar and placed her onto my lap backwards. She had to pull herself back together, so she moved slowly. Her pussy was soaking wet and had tightened right back up. My dick seemed to be a perfect fit inside of her vaginal canal. I fucked her from underneath her and she just held on to my neck for dear life. Unlike last time I decided to give her a break. I took it slow. I didn't pound her pussy this time, I asked her if she minded if I took my time with her pussy and she shook her head yes as she enjoyed my slow strokes. I gave her small bites on her back and neck. She came and moaned at the same time. Feeling herself about to have another orgasm she started to go ham on

my dick, she bounced up and down on my erect dick. As she moved her hips in an up and down motion she grabbed the handles of the chair and watched herself in the mirror as if she was enjoying watching her work.

Feeling myself getting weak and ready to explode, I had to pull it together. I wanted her to cum one more time. After I got that big nut then I could release mines. She turned to have her back towards my chest and bent all the way over to grab my ankles and tightened up her pussy muscles and bounced her plump ass cheeks on my dick. Not being able to hold it in for too much longer, she changed her position. Once she sat straight up on my meat and threw her head back over my shoulder. It was something as simple as feeling her dreads lay over my shoulder onto my back that turned me on. I heard her say "Oh shit I'm about to cum again poppy." Once her hot cum ran down on me was when I let loose. I couldn't hold it in any longer. As I came she watched me and smiled, it was like she enjoyed the sight.

She sat there still on my lap as I jerked at my release. She just stared at me and smiled while shaking her head. "You were amazing baby doll," I told her and she laughed and told me that it was all me that bought all of that out of her. She

tried to play the shy role but I had just witnessed this good girl go bad right before my very eyes. Just to think I was going to pass this piece of pussy up. This good girl went totally bad for me and released all of her juices on me. I guess I'll have to add Armani to the roaster of 'Love Slaves' because I'm about to hit this ass once more in the shower and she has no clue! (Until next time)

Chapter 6
Death Has Its Way Of Changing People

That night in Vegas changed everything between Armani and myself for the better. Instead of it turning into a continuous sexcapade between the two of us, we became the best of friends. I came home and told Raven about this wonderful woman that I met while out of town. I left out the part about us having sex, but I allowed Raven to meet Armani and I shared her story with her. Raven had a caring a warm spirit so I knew that she would fall in love with her just as I did. Well I knew that Armani still had feelings for me and wanted to be that leading lady in my life, but she chose to respect Raven and her position as my wife.

Raven and Armani began to become very close to one another. While I was at work they found several things to occupy their time. They did lots of shopping, movies and dinner dates. My friend was becoming something like my wife's companion and I was starting to feel a certain kind of way about it.

Leaving the gym for a half a day to go home and surprise Raven for a date somewhat seemed to be the wrong thing to do, once I got home. While pulling into my neighborhood, I decided to call Armani and check on her but to my surprise I got no answer. As I pulled my pepsi blue whip into my driveway, I noticed that Armani's car was out front. Raven's car was gone so I just assumed that they were out somewhere together.

Walking into the house I immediately began to strip out of my clothes to go and hop in the shower. As I walked towards the bedroom I could hear the radio playing from that direction. I slowed down and began to listen, I could hear two people talking but couldn't catch the voices. Creeping towards the door as if I was a intruder there, as I approached the door I placed my ear to the door panel and couldn't believe what I heard. My ears had to be deceiving me. I couldn't be hearing things right. My heart began to pound as my head also throbbed like never before. This couldn't be happening to me, or was this what I deserved?

Dear little black book...

Reaching for the door handle seemed like it took me 24 hours to make a connection.
Stepping into the room made me think about how this was once the intimate place of
Raven and I. While allowing my mouth to drop to the floor, I couldn't believe my eyes. There was Raven lying on her back with a red teddy on while Armani sucked on her breast as if she was looking to receive milk. Raven moaned lightly and threw her head from side to side as if she was enjoying the pleasure that she was receiving. Armani then began to play in "My pussy." This was my pussy that she was violating. She knew exactly what she was doing. She acted as if she was a nigga. While playing in Raven's play box, Raven closed her eyes and moved with Armani's fingers. "Yes baby!" Raven said in a louder tone. "Play in your pussy mommy, bring that nut out of me." Armani worked my pussy over. She dugged deep and not only did Raven cum but she began to squirt all over everything. I stood speechless until Armani pulled out her strap-on in an attempt to enter into my wife. No longer filled with anger, I was now filled with a kind of rage. It was now jealousy. I was jealous and mad as a bitch! I was livid! Without saying a word, I walked over and pushed Armani to the side with an envious motion

and threw the fake dick across the room. I pulled my rock hard dick out of my Lo boxers and looked into Raven's eyes and asked her in a serious tone, "So you was just gonna give my pussy away?" With fear and lust all in her eyes she said nothing, this pissed me off even more. With a displeased look on my face I then looked over at Armani and smirked as she was sitting there with her fingers inside of her pussy. My anger went to rage and the rage then went to jealousy and now to confusion. My emotions were all over the place. I was no longer upset. I now found myself wanting my dick inside of my wife and my tongue inside of Armani's juice box.

Looking at Raven as she looked to enjoy seeing Armani play with herself. I called Armani over to me as I teased Raven with my fingers digging inside of pussy. Raven rubbed her titties as I played in her pussy and Armani watched us both. Armani and Raven both wore sexy ass heels that strapped up their legs and I knew right then that I wanted them both, right then and there. As I dug into the walls of my wife, Armani walked over to Raven and kissed her so passionately that they turned me on. I again got jealous and tried to reach for Armani. Before I could reach her she reached over and grabbed for my dick. She had a grip that demanded my dick to stay on hard. As I

slowed down with playing in Raven's pussy, she seemed to want the shine back on her. She pushed me onto the bed, just hard enough to get my attention. As my body hit the bed Raven kissed my lips and then hopped on my dick. She rode my dick like she missed it, while Armani seemed to get a bit jealous as she watched. Raven stuck her tongue out towards Armani and said in an authoritative tone "Feed my nigga Doll Face, and feed him good."

Without hesitation Armani did what Raven demanded of her; she came and sat her sweet suckle pussy dead on my face. Without second thought my tongue just started to fight with her second set of lips. Her pussy tasted as sweet as honey. The more I ate her pussy, the harder Raven rode my dick. I don't know which one I enjoyed the most. I drank Armani's juices as Raven spilled all of hers on my stiffened dick. They tag teamed me because now that Raven came all over my dick, she was ready to feed me as well. They hit the switch-a-roo on me. You would have thought that they were WWE Wrestlers the way that they tagged each other in.

Right before Raven climbed onto my face she started to lick all of Armani's juices off of my face with enjoyment. While Raven licked the

juices off of my beard, Armani deep throated my dick like never before. I was in heaven, when at one time I was one to look down on threesomes before. I now had the best of both worlds and I wouldn't trade this duo for nothing in the world. Raven sat on her throne facing Armani and told me "Bae, you better eat this pussy better than you ate hers. Drink all of my fucking juices you nasty fuckin bastard. I tried to give that bitch her turn first but she didn't know what to do with this pussy monster." The nastier Raven talked, the hornier I had gotten. She knew that I loved that nasty shit, and she served me the shit that I liked. Once again the games began.

Armani rode my dick backwards and then after she came she turned around on my dick. When she turned around on my dick she then faced Raven and began playing with Raven's bare breast as I fucked her with my strong tongue. My tongue game was real. Not to brag but I knew what the fuck I was doing with my mouth piece. I drove Raven fucking crazy because as I fucked her with my tongue, I also fingered her to make her climax harder than before. Armani rode the fuck out of my dick as she sucked Raven's finger as if it was my dick. Once they had their way with me and came all over my dick and face, Raven went down and finished me off by making me

burst down deep into her throat. As I released in her mouth, she got up and ran the shower water.

All three of us did a repeat in the shower, and the second time seemed more intense as the first. It was something about the hot beads of water hitting our skin that sent a pleasure through the body. With their wet hair in their faces, they looked sexy as any supermodel and as provocative as any porn star known to man. I had to be the luckiest man in the world to have both of the baddest bitches in the game at the same damn time. These bitches made me love them even more. I had to spark up some of my skunky stuff to get my mind right because without even realizing it they had just rocked my world. (Until next time)

I had to have been living a dream. My feelings for Armani had grown more heavily but because of the relationship of her and Raven, I tried to put some of those feelings to the side to save Raven's feelings. But as I sat here and watched the two of them laid up on each of my arms, I knew that this wouldn't be a last time for the three of us!

This having two old-ladies was too good to be true, or so it seemed. Everything was seeming to be going smooth for about 3 months. It began to get harder and harder to hide my deeper feelings for

Armani, but I didn't much try to hide it now because we were all open with it. This love thing that the three of us had was something like living the "American Dream." Any man that wouldn't want this, had to have a pussy between his legs. I was loving every minute of it, we had an odd relationship but it worked for us. When alone you could tell that Armani yearned to have me all to herself but she also loved the variety that Raven and I gave her. She catered to me just as much as Raven did and it was like they often competed with each other for me. They didn't have to compete with one another because I loved them and appreciated them both. I valued these two women with everything in me and wouldn't trade them for any other women in this world. They had it all, everything that I needed they provided me with. They had their moments where they pleasured each other without me, and vice versa. I no longer became enraged at the thought of sharing my wife with Armani because they never told me no. If I ever wanted to join in, all I had to do was just that. Sometimes I just enjoyed the sight of both of my women pleasuring each other. We bought toys and things, we did many different things to keep our relationship spiced up. Our life was different but if others did it like us there would be much less infidelity in a lot of these relationships today!

On a Friday the day of Ramone's first lightweight fight, Armani was supposed to be going

home only to change clothes. She never made it to his fight and this worried both Raven and I. We both tried calling her cell phone but our calls went unanswered. This wasn't like Armani at all. The three of us had begun to do everything together. I became upset with thinking that maybe she tried to step out on Raven and I. I was more over protective of Armani then I was of Raven and I couldn't explain why. Raven was my number 1 but because I also often figured that Armani would soon leave because of playing second to Raven, but not thinking that It would happen so soon. I became angry and Raven knew it.

"Calm down baby. Maybe something has happened to her," Raven said as she hooked a u-turn in the middle of the street to head straight to Armani's crib.

Something wasn't right and I could feel it. It was as if we were connected. I could feel her pain within me. I couldn't quite put my hands on it but I knew that I had a bad feeling about this one.

Pulling up at Armani's condo, her car was parked up front. Something just wasn't adding up. Preparing myself to cut her off without second thought at the thought of her being there with another nigga or even another bitch. I was ready and there was no turning back if she was doing dirt. I expressed to Raven that we were done with Armani for good if she

was up to no good. She knew how I acted at the thought of anyone doing wrong by me. No matter how much dirt I had done, I simply couldn't take it being done to me. Raven hesitated at first. She didn't do drama well, but she knew that Armani was her friend and her lover. She couldn't fathom the thought of anything ever happening to her. Her heart pounded as I opened my car door. I came around to her side of the car and opened her door. She stood up, but as soon as she built up the courage to get out of the car, her legs buckled. I felt as if I could not hold her up. By the grace of God, I held her up as she drank some of her drink trying to gain composure. It was as if she knew that we were walking into something that we weren't ready for. I struggled to keep her straight up. She was weak at the knees. After she asked the Lord for a second wind, he gave her just that. We continued to stand and pray as she felt her strength replenish in her body.

Walking towards her house was the first of the harder tasks that was set forth simply for her. Raven rang the doorbell twice out of a courtesy and then when she got no response was when she used her personal key. Being as if Armani knew that the doctors only gave her a set amount of time to live, she decided to give us a key to have for emergencies.

Turning the knob after entering, the key seemed like the wrong thing to do. It seemed as if all

79

of the air in my lungs had just left my body. This was no time for me to bitch up now. I had to see what was going on with my lady. There was no sign of her on the first level of the house so we headed up to the second level. Her door was closed and this made my heart throb instantly. I was sure that she was in there with some other nigga but I had to face the facts. Before I went to enter the bedroom, it was as if every moment that I shared with her had just flashed before my eyes. From the first time that I laid eyes on her at the lounge in Vegas, I fell for her that night. It was just something different about her, she and Raven were alike and like none other. My mind then traveled to the first time that her, Raven and I had our first encounter together. I loved this lady with everything in me. I said a brief prayer and then looked over at Raven who stood there with obvious fear in her eyes. I kissed her forehead and then opened the bedroom door to see what looked like Armani laying there peacefully resting. A sigh of relief came over me as I rushed to her bedside. I just needed to kiss her face. We looked around the room and everything looked normal. I went straight for Armani and Raven went over to the nightstand that sat next to the bed and picked up a piece of paper. I bent over to kiss her head and realized that she was ice cold. Not thinking nothing of it, my natural reaction was to pull the covers up onto her body. But her body laid there stiff, she didn't budge. With the gasp for air that Raven tried to catch startling me, it made me turn my

attention over to Raven. That's when I saw the stream of tears escaping her eyes at a rapid pace made me realize that things weren't looking to good. Raven dropped the damp piece of paper and rushed over to our lovers side and began pumping on her chest to recover her from the impossible. Once she had no luck with reviving her she screamed at me for me to call 911. It was like I was frozen, this couldn't be. My lover couldn't be dead, please let it all be a horrific dream. I couldn't get my mind to function right. I couldn't remember the code to unlock my phone. Then I couldn't remember the number to 911. I was just all to pieces, I was just distraught. Why my baby? Why did she have to leave me in dismay? Before I knew it Raven had snatched my phone out of my hand and made the call herself. She had given me looks of death as if she thought that I was being funny. She didn't realize that this love that I had for Armani was unconditional. Not one soul would be able to repair the damage that this was sure to do to my heart. This agony that I was feeling was a hurt that I couldn't describe. It was a devastating pain and I wished it on no one. Raven was my wife but I felt as if I needed her and Armani both to complete me.

I looked down at the piece of paper in my hand as the words over clouded my head. I managed to focus on the text before me and it read:

She had no intentions… no intentions on caring so much... loving... giving... seeing... just existing… then enters HE... He showed her that she was a woman so she cares what he thinks. He showed her his heart so she loves. He gives her his all. She does the same in return. He shows her that she is somebody so she believes him and begins. He gives her life so she lives. Her life is now his and his is hers. He loves. She loves. Then he gives her HER. She does the same as he. They all share each other. He hurts. THEY hurt. He smiles. THEY smile. He's Her's. THEY'RE his. THEY all are one. ONE life. ONE heartbeat. ONE soul... happy... loving... living... SHE is we and he YOU. Forever was always the goal. And forever will be reached even if it's not in this lifetime. I will forever live on in YOUR HEARTS. Until HE and SHE reunites with ME in OUR spirits…

Thankful for the love that the two of you have given to me. You have showed me how to love once again and for that I have truly lived. Speedy, from the moment that I saw you in that boxing ring as a little girl I already knew that I loved you. When I saw you in Vegas, I had no intentions on loving you this deeply but you made it so easy. I dreamed of US being ONE and then when you gave me Raven, I had to have you both! At first I saw it as an opportunity to have you without having to sneak and be with you but then I met and fell in love with my dear heart Raven. You two are heaven sent and I thank God for giving me life again with Y'ALL. I love the two of you and

please never forget me and the love that WE shared!

Love,
Armani Bridges

P.S.
Don't you two ever try to replace me because NO ONE will EVER add up xoxoxoxoxo

Chapter 7
Things Will Never Be The Same

After saying our last good byes to the love of our life, things were just not the same anymore. Raven and I both buried ourselves in our work. Raven had been writing more than ever and had been working on a special project that she shared with no one. She often told me that she wanted it to be a surprise. We were both hurting very badly but tried to play like we were ok. We hardly talked much anymore and our sex game was beginning to be non-existent. It just wasn't the same without our Armani and it was very apparent to the both of us. We were always in our own zones. If we were home, Raven spent most of the nights in her office and I stayed down in my man cave. There was no more togetherness with us. Something had to be done. She focused on her writing and I put my all into the training at the gym. I worked with all of my clients but my main focus was Ramone. I had other trainers in the gym that helped me train but I let no one train Ramone but myself. He was my little piece of greatness and I was determined to make sure that he was 10 times better than myself. He was just about there. He was a prize to watch.

His parents left Ramone in my hands because they saw the difference that I made in his life. His mind was on his boxing and also Kenya, the honey that he had met in Vegas. She was really feeling Ramone and his feelings were mutual. She had a few more months left in her schooling and then she had plans on relocating from California to Virginia to be with him. They both were saddened by the news of Armani, because they had met her while we were in Vegas and they saw the love that I had for her. Ramone stayed close by me because he could see the genuine love that Raven and I had for her.

Kenya came to see Ramone's first fight so she was here when we were going through it behind Armani's death. She was a big piece of support for all of us. Ramone found himself a good one and he appreciated her just as such.

Life was life, not too much happiness was displayed between Raven and I. I saw a separation in our near future, and I know that it had crossed her mind as well. Neither of us dared to speak the words but our actions showed that it was an option. It was until Ramone managed to get both Raven and I in the same location. Somehow he got us both at our favorite restaurant and asked us not to say anything. He just wanted us to listen to him. He was stern with us and broke things down to us that made us feel ashamed that we had been neglecting one another. While we were both going through the same pain, we

needed to lean on one another and go through it together. He turned to me and asked in a serious tone if it was ok for him to give up on his fighting dream?

"Hell no it's not," was my reply. Then he asked Raven in a more caring tone, "Dukes (that was what he called her) is it ok if I take your work that you've been working on and destroy it like it's no big deal"? Raven gave him a stank look that said it all. "Ok then if these things are important to you guys then why isn't the love that you two have worked so hard to maintain all these years?" Ramone asked. "Y'all know that I look at the two of you as my second set of parents, and it bothers me that you two are dying inside. Y'all need each other but you're letting the hurt separate you two. I know that Mani wouldn't want to see you guys like this. She's probably turning over in her grave at how you two have been carrying on down here. Pop's, I need you to be here for Dukes. She needs you man! And the same for you Dukes, get back to loving one another. Y'all were my idol couple and it's now hurting me to see the two of you acting like this. Is this really what love is about because if so then I don't want to love anymore. As you walk in the doors of the gym, the both of you have the biggest picture plastered on the wall with the words "KEEP FIGHTING" but you're not living by that." Ramone's big eyes started to get filled up with his tears. They tried to creep out but then Raven looked over at her husband and told him that she loved him and "I want to keep fighting with you." I beat Ramone to the punch, as thorough of a man that I was, my woman had just broke me down. My tears

flowed but it was as if I was cleansing my soul. The two of us knew what we had to do and that was to get back to love once again. Ramone saved our marriage and for that he would forever be my favorite fighter!

The healing had become much easier with the two of us doing it together. We talked more and began to get back to the basics of our love. Ramone presented us with a canvas of a beautiful painting that he had taken and painted himself of Raven, Armani and myself and it was certainly a masterpiece. It was perfect, it captured her true beauty. It gave us some of the healing that we needed. We hung it in the foyer and saw it as soon as we entered into our home. Armani was still with us, she lived through us and it made our lives much more worth living. Happiness showed its beauty in our relationship once again and the love was stronger than ever. We made it our business to devote our Sundays as family day. We would go out to the grave and talk to our love and also present her with freshly picked flowers and cleaned off the old ones. We were getting back to us, and it was a beautiful and relieving thing. We thanked Ramone every chance that we got and was sure to make sure how grateful that we were for him to care so much.

While coming close to our healing with Armani's death was when it was our turn to be there for Ramone as he was for us. Even though he looked

at Raven and I as his second set of parents, he had a close bond with his biological parents as well. We were all close and were all there for Ramone as his support system. Marcy and LaShawn were his parents and they were working towards putting Marcy through school. She was in her last year of school to be a mortician so LaShawn went out and got a part time gig, to make sure that they were straight. I commend him for being a hardworking man that only wanted the best for his family. He started to work a security gig at a nightclub in the city nearest to them. It was late hours but the pay made it worth it.

Everything was working out for the best and coming together in their favor. They watched as their son developed into the next Speedy Wright and was now getting paid for his gift of boxing. They were so proud of Ramone for his dedication and his hard work that he displayed to the world. Marcy was holding down her teaching career and also a full-time student. LaShawn was a firefighter by day and a security guard at Dreams nightclub by night. He had a natural instinct to look after others. He was a no non-sense type of guy but he didn't like confusion. He tried to always avoid problems with anyone, he was one to always want to see others happy but on the other hand he was never to be mistaken as a punk. He was about his shit, he always wanted people to be protected. This was his gift that he was given by God, to protect. But his gift cursed him in the long run and

changed the lives of his loved ones. Once his shift had ended at the club after they worked on clearing the parking lots, he was walking to his car and that was when he witnessed a girl and a guy in the back side of the parking lot arguing. He could hear the slur in the man's voice as they fussed about a man trying to dance on the female. He seemed to have been upset about the girl not moving away fast enough. He mentioned that she made him look stupid in front of his boys so he was pissed of with her. "Nobody makes QB look stupid bitch, you must have wanted that nigga up on your ass. I don't appreciate that shit Jade, you trying to play a nigga right? Now you gotta pay." The girl had a disturbed look on her face like she knew what was to come next. It was as if he was known for beating her ass. While LaShawn was off of the clock, he could have just got in his car and went home to his family. LaShawn felt as if he had to help the small framed woman. Walking towards the couple while shaking his head and sighing, he said out loud "Lord don't let me have to fuck a nigga up out here tonight." When the girl's attention turned to LaShawn walking towards them, she shook her head as she was trying to warn LaShawn. He saw the apparent fear in her eyes so instead of LaShawn taking the girls hint, he wanted to rescue her. Seeing his girlfriend's attention on something other than him, he turned in the direction of her trance. "Oh shit bro, you trying to play save a hoe out this bitch" shouted the drunk boyfriend in a slurred tone. LaShawn laughed

because he seen tough drunk guys every night that he worked at the club. The only difference was that the guys inside of the club went through a pat down. "Just let her go on about her business homeboy and y'all talk about this shit tomorrow once you're no longer angry and have a clear head" say's LaShawn. The drunk man laughed and turned to the half dressed woman beside him, she was shaking. "No Mr. I'm ok, you can go on about your way. I'm trying to help you, he is not going to harm me" says the lady in fear. She pleaded with LaShawn to not come any further but he kept on towards them and that was when the drunk man started reaching into his car for something. Meeting LaShawn part of the way and talking shit he says "Listen my nigga this is not the shit that you want. I'm not afraid of those bars nigga. I'll go back behind a fuck boy like you that don't know how to mind his fucking business. I've warned you my nigga, so you can't say that you haven't been warned." The girl hollers and cries saying "No QB, come on baby. I'm sorry baby let's go home" she begged but then LaShawn laughed at the coward. This was a big mistake because that was when the drunk man went in his waistline revealing what he had gotten out of the car. QB looked at LaShawn with off look in his eyes and before Lashawn knew what was coming to him, the man opened fire on him in close range and blew his brains all over the parking lot. The girl screamed as she saw his brains splatter everywhere. The sound of her scream irritated the

drunken man, he turned towards the female and he then shot at her from where he stood. With six shots in her direction, the man had taken her down to the ground. Where she was hit couldn't be seen at that moment. Snapping out of his crazed rage he realized what he had just done, he looked at the two bodies that he had just taken down. He didn't know which way to turn. He looked at LaShawn's lifeless body and then looked at the direction of the young lady and ran her way. As he ran her way he heard sirens getting closer to them, he ignored the sirens and fell to the ground asking the young lady to hold on. "Don't die on me baby, I'm sorry. What about our baby that you're carrying? I need you here. I lost my cool baby. I'm sorry. I told you that I would never hurt you again, baby please hold on." At that moment was when a slew of cop cars along with the firetruck and ambulance. LaShawn died instantly and by the time the police had gotten to the female victim, QB was still there holding her while crying. Right before Jade took her last breath she looked at the officer and said "He shot us, that man was just trying to protect me from him and he shot him." After those last words she said was when her eyes rolled back in her head and she was gone. Right there in the arms of her killer she and their unborn child had just taken her last breath.

With getting the statement that they needed to know about the crime that he had just committed from the murder victim, he was read his rights and placed in

handcuffs. They spotted the murder weapon lying in the middle of the street that also contained the fingerprints of Mr. Quincy QB Barker. QB cried a remorseful cry but it was too late for cries, those cries could not bring back these innocent people.

LaShawn's protective instincts had cost him his life. His life was taken prematurely and the hand's of a drunken four time felon. His fire fighter division had agreed to take the responsibility of breaking the news to his family. They knew of LaShawn and it saddened them because they could speak for his character. He was a great person and a dedicated worker that loved his family.

At 5:30 am was when the captain of the fire and rescue squad arrived at the house that LaShawn shared with his wife and son. This was definitely a visit that they always dreaded, but this time it was a little harder. LaShawn was well known and well loved in the community. Marcy jumped up when she heard the knocks at the door. The knocks got louder and harder and frightened both Ramone as well as Marcy. Grabbing her house coat and heading to the door as Ramone followed behind on his mother's heels. Ramone had a bad feeling and knew that this late night visit was because of his father. They both wore looks for fright on their faces. After opening the door that separated the calm from the storm was like a world wind had just taken over their home. While

Captain Leon Marshall who was a black man that found a liking to LaShawn, he watched LaShawn from the time that he entered the academy and he was blessed to witness all of his accomplishments. Captain Marshall knew Marcy and Ramone personally and couldn't find the words to say to break the news to them Looking into their worried eyes brought tears to his eyes. Obviously choked up, Ramone was the first to break the silence. "What's wrong Mr. Marshall, is my dad ok?" Shaking his head no and then finding the courage to tell them what happened seemed to be the hardest thing that he had ever had to do. They're mouths dropped and Marcy asked him to repeat what he had just said because couldn't have heard him correctly. She knew that LaShawn was later than normal getting home but there had to have been a mistake she thought. The tears wouldn't even fall from her eyes as she listened to the story of what happened. She only focused on Ramone and how he would react. He loved and admired his father like the typical son did his father but Ramone felt strongly about family. Marcy was hurting but it relieved her knowing that he died with doing what he loved to do and that was to protect others. She was saddened by the news but she felt as if she had to find and display strength for her son. Watching the reaction of Ramone made Captain Marshall cry even harder.

Marcy prayed as they cried and asked for strength, she needed strength to get through this to be there for

her son. The more she talked to the Lord, the calmer she had become. Her inner strength was building but this frightened Ramone because he didn't see his mother mourn as he thought that she would. He watched as she prayed and began to pray with her.

Marcy worried about Ramone and how this would affect him and his life. She cried but she made sure that it was when he wasn't around. She had several sleepless days and nights. Her job gave her a leave with pay but her schooling had begun to start failing. She just couldn't concentrate on her loss. She was a believer in the Lord but she started to question his actions. "Why do you take the good one's Lord, why my baby," she asked. The bond of Ramone and Marcy had gotten tighter and Raven made it her business to keep Marcy occupied as much as she could. Kenya was truly the companion that Ramone needed. She flew in as soon as she heard what happened. Ramone made his mind of that everything that he did he would do it for his father. He wanted to make his father proud and to keep his legacy going.

Ramone went hard in the gym, he kept focused and kept me on my toes. I admired his strength. He used what the devil meant to destroy him and turned it into what recreated him. He missed his father dearly and he never went a day without talking to him, but he was now living to leave a legacy! He took his anger, hurt and pain out on his opponents. He was

undefeated and he was forming into his greatness right before my eyes. He wouldn't quit, no matter what obstacles were thrown his way. I learned a lot from Ramone, and his strength helped me heal from Armani's death and I owed it all to him. He was my hero, the roles had reversed. He was no longer the little guy that I met at the gym, he was now a grown man.

Kenya was blessed with the opportunity to graduate early and this gave her the opportunity to move to be with her lover. It took her no time to get her career started and they continued staying with his mother and helped her with the bills. Marcy was able to catch back up with her schooling and still maintain the bills, because of Kenya and Ramone. Life had seemed to be getting back to normal as possible for each of them coming from their hard times.

Chapter 8 Finding One's Self Once Again

Life was beginning to be a beautiful thing once more. It was like I was finally able to see through the fog again. Life was good! Raven and I were back and better than ever. She still worked on this special project that she found to be important to keep a surprise. She continued to go with me to each of my doctor's appointments. I was now learning to deal with and accept what the doctor's saw on their fancy medical machines. I kind of felt like Armani. I was just going to love and live my life like it's golden. I started to lose more and more of my brain functions, they became more noticeable to me, but I made the most of it. That was where Raven came in at and she played her part. What I forgot she made sure that I remembered. There hadn't been many journals entries since my sweet Armani was taken from us. I wasn't too mad at that either. Life now appeared to be more golden than ever. I found myself searching for Armani in different women that I would see at the grocery stores, gas stations, restaurants, just everywhere. I imagined that God would bring her back to me just in another form. Some way, somehow I was determined to find her again.

I found myself relapsing back into the old me the more that I missed Armani. Raven had a book convention out of town that she would be attending for the next three days. I was a free man with no plans, but I was determined to make some plans. Raven hesitated on leaving me home alone because she felt as if I would need her. I advised her that I would be fine and I told her that Ramone would be around if I needed someone.

While she was gone I did hardly nothing, on the sunday that Raven was to return was when I decided to hit the streets. There was an all black party that was supposed to have been jumping in the city tonight. I hit the mall earlier that day and copped me an all black fit and was ready to bless the city with my presence. While never wanting to arrive at the party too early I took a ride through the city while smoking on my herbs. Smoking that hemp seemed to be the only thing to take the stress of the world away. Sex and weed were my outlets. No one really understood my struggles in this world, not even my wife. I stressed when things were good and also when things were bad because the fact still remained true that my life was sometimes a blur to me. Tomorrow really wasn't promised to anyone but let these doctors tell it, I really didn't have much more living to do. I was a true believer in the man upstairs but I also had to admit that I am a natural born worrier. I worried about everything, in my eyes something could always go

wrong. To me it made sense to think this way because if you expected the worse and hoped for the best then either way it was less disappointment.

Rolling and listening to that Jay and Big mix, I let them put me in my zone. I felt as if I was the man all of a sudden! This haze that my mind was in had me feeling like I was on top of the world. I was ready to show the world my all tonight. Pulling up at Roger B's and seeing that there was hardly any parking on the whole street let me know that I was in the right place. Everybody was riding clean out here. Seeing a few familiar cars on the scene let me know what type of night that it was about to become. I circled the block a time or two just to check out the views and to make sure that I got a good vibe about the environment. I always did this just to make sure that everything was on the up and up, and if I ever got a bad vibe I never proceeded with the plans. The vibe was cool so I parked and stepped out the whip, I had to look myself over and loved what I saw. I felt good about myself tonight. Looking down at my black Gucci loafers that matched the belt that sat in my black linen pants and my black v-neck t-shirt that showed off my gym dedication. I'm normally not a stuck on myself type of nigga but tonight I was on my grown man shit and it felt good. Before leaving the car I sprayed my Gucci Guilty smell wells and then locked up the whip after grabbing my phone. "Let's get it nigga" I said to myself in a confident tone. It felt good to feel like

myself again, I'm a humble ass nigga but from time to time I had to hop on my own dick for a few.

Walking up to the door of the establishment had a nigga hyped. The DJ was scratching and pumping the old school rap. Standing at the door checking Id's was a young lady looking to be every bit of 21, she grinned as soon as I hit the door. "Hey Speedy" she said in a flirty tone. Shorty was twirling her hair and batting her eyelashes as if she knew me. I spoke but at the same time tried to figure out if I knew her and how she knew my nickname. She looked at me as if she was waiting for me to say something, when I didn't say much was when she smacked her lips and shouted "Oh, so you don't know nobody now?" I smiled at her and with a high look and a head tilt I tried hard to try to remember. Looking at her for a little while and then apologizing saying "I'm sorry baby please forgive me, please blame it on my mind and not my heart. I forget a lot nowadays", while shaking my head at myself because I really didn't know who shorty was. She looked agitated at me and says "Damn so our night together meant nothing to you, that's fucked up." Without trying to, I really put shorty into her feelings just that quick. Not wanting to tell her my business about my health condition, I just looked at her with a sincere look and told her that I smoked too much. She co-signed by saying "Yes, because you had me Johnny Blazed that night. I'm Bridget. I met you at Lia and Sam's bridal shower and

we had a good night that night. You licked me from the front to the back and I have been trying to find someone that could add up to your head game ever since." After hugging her and giving her my business card she stamped my hand and let me inside of the party without paying. I smiled to myself and walked through the packed spot just like I was the man.

As I began to walk through the club the perfect song started to play, just for me! Walk through by Rich Homie blared through the speakers. I screwed my face up as I caught the beat. Bobbing my head as if he was talking about me!

Singing... I be feeling like the man when I walk thru.. I ain't stunting what you saying when I walk thru...I got all these hoes staring when I walk thru... Had to make a few bands on the walk thru... Watch me, watch me, watch me walk thru... I done made a few bands on the walk thru...I done made a few bands on the walk thru... People I don't know now I don't talk to... Me and Problem in this bitch, he a boss too, sitting at the round table making boss moves... I done walked thru with Gucci on my feet, who got more money, you or me? Imma walk thru usually, with my niggas, best believe I got dat tool on me... I done snuck past security, What The Fuck do you need glasses, just you see, me... When I'm coming full speed...Got dat V12 coming. .. And imma jump the fence if I see 12 coming... Even if I was blind

I could still smell money... Can't trust no outsiders, they could tell on me...I'm the alphabet boy cause I keep a L on me... I smoke good, throwing up my set in yo hood... Nigga ... I be feeling like the man when I walk thru...

Rocking to my theme song as I flowed through the club with a slight grin and a little bit of a cocky grit. I really felt like the man when I walked thru! I looked like money and I knew it, looking down at my Gucci shoes and then back up at my Gucci belt knowing that I was one of the flyest niggas in the club. If not the flyest. I was far from conceited, but hell yeah a nigga is cocky as a mutha fucka! I had a reason to be shit, I'm a black nigga with plenty of bread. The most important part of it that I'm proud about is that I've made every bit of my bread legally. Nobody gave me shit but a chance! I did this shit and I have a lot of shit to be proud of. Even the hustling nigga's out here in the streets respected me and my grind and hustle.

When I was in the boxing ring I put on for my city. I carried my city, Hampton was on my back! My nigga's saw and respected real, and real was what I have always claimed to be. I had the love from all nigga's and my females loved a nigga as well. Tonight was no different. They showed a nigga love! I was a hometown hero in their eyes. I could never not show love in return because these same people that showed me love while I was in the ring are still

showing me the same love at the gym. The hometown dudes brought their sons to join and some of them have also joined themselves. It was all love for the kid!

The first one to stop me and spread the love was Rozlyn Britt from Rip Rap Road. Sexy Roz is what I called her. She was just as sexy now as she was back then. I used to want to get in between Roz's thighs so bad back then, she played hard to get. I didn't have the patience for the chase back then especially when all I wanted was the ass. She stood about 5'7 and about 170 pounds. Baby was thick in the waist and cute in the face. She was a bad one! Every nigga in the city of Hampton was wanting a piece of Rozlyn back then but she gave nigga's no play. That's what made me respect her even more, she could have been the biggest hoe out there but she kept her shit tight. She didn't choose the school jock, which she could have but instead she chose just a regular joe. He didn't sell drugs, didn't play sports, he was just a regular cool ass nigga that stayed to himself. This made me look at her different when I saw that she chose Breon and stuck by his side for a long time.

As she approached me, she stood back and looked me over with a smile. She showed all of her teeth as she looked at me. I couldn't help but to smile back at her. Sexy Roz was looking better than ever,

she aged like a champ. She looked every bit of 25 and she was well into her late 30's. Her body was still tight, waist small and titties were plump and juicy and her ass still stuck out like a Georgia peach. She wrapped her hands around my waist and laid her head on my chest while in the embrace. She smelled like a flower and her lips were poppin. She made me want to attack her and be all on that but I had to remember that I was a married man.

"Speedy, how are you love?! I haven't seen you in years. I heard that you were doing your thing out there in the ring. I'm so proud of you man, not too many of y'all cats did much with y'all lives. But you did and that says a lot. I knew that you would make something of yourself, because you were just different to me. Remember when you used to try to get a me? I wanted you so bad but I also knew that you had your little fan club and I cared not to join that club. I wanted my own man. I didn't want to share you with anyone. I refused, so no matter how much I wanted you, I had to want you from afar Speedy."

I looked at her as she confessed how she wanted me and thought back to those days and times. I didn't think that Sexy Roz wanted a nigga like me, but as she just said she wanted a nigga. I could have made her my girl. She was a good girl back then. Looking her from head to toe I licked my lips and rubbed my hands together and asked her, "So what's

good witcha Sexy Roz? How have you been"? She blushed when I called her Sexy Roz, she played that shy role as she used to do. "Nothing much Speedy, I remember you used to always call me that. I have to admit I loved when you called me that. I've thought of you over the years, but couldn't believe that I never ran back into you again. I just moved back from Atlanta, I moved out there with Breon. Breon and I were still together up until the last 6 months. We were 10 years deep into our relationship when I found out that Breon had been fucking his barber. That nigga was a fucking faggot Speedy. This shit broke my heart into so many pieces. My fucking old man was into fucking men, that shit is fucking disgusting. I tried to kill that nigga when I caught him in my car while his barber was giving him head." The look on her face told me that she had just replayed the scene in her head.

My mouth dropped wide open at the thought of that dude Breon messing with men. "Wow, I can't believe that dude went that way, messing with niggas man. Damn, I'm sorry that you went through that Roz. But other than that how have you been? How has sexy Roz really been, fuck that fuck boy shit. How are you outside of that?" She sighed a long sigh and smiled and said "I'm better Speedy, I'm not gonna lie to you. That Breon shit had me fucked up and on some get back shit. I almost killed that nigga. That's some really nasty shit. I gave this nigga so much of

my life and this is how he repays me. I tried to slit that nigga's throat. He lucky that my daughter walked in because he was a dead bitch! I gave this nigga 3 kids and all along he was playing me and then on top of that this faggot is fucking niggas. I would have rather him cheat on me with a group of bitches, but this nigga starts fucking with the dooky shoots. UGH, that's just some nasty shit. When I thought about him putting me in danger, I turned red and saw red and almost took that nigga out. I felt like I wanted to shoot this nigga dead in his temple with my 9mm. The grace of God saved his bitch ass. But anyways, enough of my damn drama. How has life been treating you, you're looking great! What ever happened to ole' girl that you were with for the longest. What's her name, uhhhh little miss priss…The stuck up acting bitch... RAVEN, that's her name! What happened to her?" I laughed so hard at Rozlyn trying to sneak diss, but little did she know my baby was doing great! Let me hit this chick with a dose of reality.

"Well little Mrs. Priss aka Raven, BKA my wife is doing wonderful! We own two businesses, and she is an author as well as a publisher. So yeah, she's great. She's definitely holdin shit down, like a boss." I left her little ass standing there looking dumb as fuck and I walked off and kept on moving through the crowd.

105

I saw a few familiar faces, threw my hands up at known niggas from other hoods. Walking towards the back of the club is where I saw my Shell Road nigga's posted up looking like a bunch of bosses. Shell Road was my block. We were some of the most well respected niggas in the city. There was us and then there was the cool ass Rip Rap and the 1135 Lincoln Park niggas. We were all some cool ass getting money ass niggas. Selling dope was the popular thing to do back in our days but I chose to go a whole separate route. I found a wall and posted up on as I drifted off into my memories.

Taking a trip down memory lane in my thought….

I lost my father and my only brother to the drug game. My brother Bryce wanted to follow in my father's footsteps so bad, he wanted to finish off my Pop's legacy since my Pop's got locked years ago. My brother was 7 years older than me and I was the smarter one of the two. He wanted to be like my father so bad, I just didn't get it. My father fathered us while he was able to but it was because of my father that my mother was killed in a drive by shooting. My father was getting that bread, that drug money. He was well respected in the streets and niggas were scared of the infamous Mozell Wright. My father rolled with heavy hitters. He only had to say one word and a nigga was zapped. I've seen some ill shit be done to niggas that tried to fuck over my pops or any nigga in

his crew. When it came to his family, he was a good nigga. But the streets had him, we didn't stand a chance. Mom was a good ass woman. She didn't work because my pops didn't want his lady to work. So she stayed home and took care of my brother and I. She didn't hound him or stress him being out in the streets. She would always tell him "Mozell remember the saying a happy wife makes a happy life" and he would tell her "Brina now you know what they say, a man that has all the time in the world, is a broke man. Now I know that you don't want no broke man, do you?" Mom would laugh because she knew that pop's made Sabrina Wright a spoiled ass brat that was used to getting her way. He just stayed on the grind. He really didn't have a lot of time for us. He got in his moods about once or twice per month where he would take us out and show us a nice time. We were straight financially and would buy us anything that we asked for but he just couldn't leave those streets alone. It had nothing to do with other women because if he was cheating on mom, we knew nothing about it. That's why mom didn't complain too much, she stayed pushing the newer whips and always kept the latest handbags and shoes. She was a gorgeous and loyal big boned woman. Momma was 5'5 and weighed 215 pounds. She was beautiful though, many slim women tried to get at my pops but it was something about my mother that he loved. He loved her size and her flaws. She did it better than half of these little skinny women. I respected that about him,

he loved my mother unconditionally and she loved him the same.

For the longest time everyone thought that I would be like my father and get a big boned woman because in my eyes my ma was the Queen of all Queens. No one did it like her. You would never catch her slipping. She kept her hair and nails done and her attire was always fly. She also kept my brother and I looking like a million bucks. Pops only wore white v-neck t-shirts and blue jeans and he kept the old school sneakers like shell toe Adidas or Nike flights. Pops was a cool ass cat and he had a lot of cats jealous of him.

I remember back on my mom's and pop's 20th wedding anniversary, my pop's took her out for a 2 day get-a-way to the Poconos. They left us with my dad's close friend Stevo and while they were gone, Stevo went to one of his lil honeys crib and she had her daughter and her niece there. Her daughter was 21 and her niece was 18 and my brother and I were 17 and 10 years old. When Stevo and his shorty went to the back, he told the two young ladies that he will hook them up and he threw them $40 a piece and they did just that. My brother and I were in this ladies house getting head and fucking these broads that we didn't even know. I was 10 years old not knowing what to do in this bitches pussy. She could tell that I didn't know what to do so she took her time and gave

Dear little black book…

Sitting on the living room couch looking at TV feeling like a grown ass man in the body of a young man. Stevo's shorty Maria walked out of her room in nothing but a bra and panty set and walked and stood in front of me. She looked and winked seductively and then looked over at her niece Brittany who had just came from out of the shower. When she looked at Brittany, Brittany shook her head at her aunt and looked at me as I looked confused. I wanted to be excited but I didn't know if I was supposed to so I played it safe. I knew nothing of playing my cards. I only knew that I was fucking a 21 year old shorty that seemed to really like me and I didn't want to mess that up. Maria then bent over in front of me and started jerking her hips in a humping motion. She looked as if she was imagining fucking me. Brittany looked pissed off and shouted out "I KNEW I SHOULDN'T HAVE TOLD YOU ABOUT THIS NIGGA'S HEAD AND DICK GAME! YOU JUST TRIFLING AUNTIE!" She smacked her lips and rolled her eyes at me and I stood up from the couch that I was on and walked over to Brittany and sat next to her and kissed her on the lips. I told her that I didn't want her aunt. "I'm happy with you Britt. You don't have to worry about her." She smiled and Maria looked dumb in the face

and told her as I tried to concentrate and fuck her from the back. I fucked her hard. The harder I fucked her the more she screamed and moaned. She came on my dick and all I felt was a heated gush of wetness where she had just had an orgasm on my dick and without warning my body began to shake and jerk. I had a bolt shoot through my whole body. It felt different from all of the other times, it had to be because of us fucking without a rubber on. This little dude shot all of my cum inside of her grown woman pussy hole and it felt damn good. As soon as I came all in her pussy and went to the bathroom to clean up was when Stevo hollered and told me that it was time to roll out. Going to the living room and kissing Brittany and told her to call me and left out. She turned me into a man that day by letting me drive into her deep tunnel without a seatbelt on. I was gone off of pussy from that day on. From a boy to a man. I had a 21 year old 'Love Slave.' I'm the man (Until next time)

Rolling through the city with Stevo had me feeling like a brand new man. Not only had I lost my virginity from a 21 year old but I was handling that shit. I hit that shit a couple of times now and she didn't want a nigga to stop. Pulling up at the corner store where my pop's and Stevo often met, I noticed my pop's sitting outside on his whip. Getting out of the car

I walked over to my pop's to give him dap and I noticed an unreadable look on his face and this made me worry. Before I could think of anything my pop's punched Stevo dead in the face and asked him "So you just gonna let my youngin run up in some slow ass broad. Word on my life I should kill your bitch ass Stevo. This is some fuck shit that you have been doing. How you gonna take my boys innocence from him so early. If I didn't fuck with you so heavy, I would take your fucking life right here and now." He looked at me and told me to get my ass in his car. Without hesitation I did what he told me to do. I was no fool. I knew that my pop's was cool but he was no one to fuck with. I was scared for Stevo, but he should have known better than to fuck with pop's.

Trying to see what was going on with my old man and Stevo but all I could see what pops up in Stevo's face. I laid my seat back and tried to drown out the thoughts of my punishment when I got home.

Drifting off into a deep sleep was when I had a dream that Maria and her niece Britt came to the house and my mother greeting them at the door. Not knowing who they were my mother opened the door and stepped onto the porch to listen to the ladies reasoning for coming to our home. Mom expecting Maria to be there to tell her something about my pops but to her surprise, Maria told her that her 21 year old niece had been fucking her 11 year old son. She also

told my mom that the last time that I fucked Britt, we fucked raw and Britt was pregnant. My mom didn't believe what she was hearing, so she called me outside on the porch and asked me if I knew them and as bad as I wanted to lie there was no need. Shaking my head yes, my mom had a disappointing look on her face. She then asked me the million dollar question. "Did you have sex with this young lady unprotected?" Shaking my head yes as I was scared to speak. My mom walked up on me and knocked the wind out of my chest. As she was about to hit me again, I saw her fist balled up and cock back and then my father pulled up on two wheels. Throwing the car in park, my pops hopped out with his pistol in hand and stomped over to Maria and gave her the look of death. Shouting, "Bitch, do we have a fuckin problem!? We must do because you're at my crib disrupting my god damn family. Bitch you must be as retarded as your child molesting ass niece. I will kill both of you bitches out this bitch! Brittany looked at me with saddened eyes and they ran off to the car and they were never seen again.

Waking up from the sound of my father's voice yelling at me saying "So you wanna be a grown man huh? You wanna fuck 21 year old bitches at 10 and 11 years old huh? Well I hope that bullshit was worth it because I'm gonna kill those bitches. Let me catch them, my word I'm gonna kill em son." Looking at my father's face let me know that he meant every word

that he was saying. Scared to death, I didn't want anyone to die and besides I liked Brittany a lot. But I knew my father so I knew better than to question him or to give him any lip about what had just been said.

15 minutes later of me and my pops sitting in his car still talking was when the police rolled up on him. That was the last time that I saw my father out in the streets. They arrested him on felony drug charges. They had been building a case on my pops and it also was rumored that Stevo had called them boys on my pops. It was an overall fucked up day from that moment on. My mom was called to come and get me. She also went off out there on the police for talking shit about her husband. My brother was left with that guilt on his conscious, because he was the one that told pops about Stevo taking us over Maria's house in the first place. That was what started the whole thing and that lead to Stevo calling the man on pops. So from there on out Bryce tried to live in my father's legacy and in less than 6 months from my father getting arrested was when mom was caught in a drive by shooting and was killed. The streets talked and the word was that it was a retaliation stunt that was called on my father. Because pops had some Southside Norfolk niggas killed, they got the next best thing to him and that was my beautiful mom.

R.I.P Sabrina Wright my angel.

From the day that my mom was killed my brother let that turn him for the worse. He wanted to fill my pops shoes but he wasn't built for that. He hustled off of my dad's name. Nigga's fronted him work but he was out here doing nigga's dirty. He sold soap as crack and some more of the old school dirty tactics. A year after my mother passed away my brother was part of a sting and they got him on plenty of felony drug and handgun charges. My dad was found dead in his jail cell about 5 years after my brother got there and my brother hated the world even his own flesh and blood so I never tried to reach out to him ever again.

Coming back to reality as someone tapped me on the shoulder.

Startled out of my trip down memory lane by the tapping on my right shoulder was my nigga Emanuel Lewton "Man Lew" from the hood. Realizing who it was brought a smile on my face. We both said in unison "MY NIGGA" and followed it up with our secret dap and handshake. "What's good my nigga?" I asked in an excited tone. I chopped it up with him for about 15 minutes and we exchanged numbers and then he peeled off and I then did another walk through of the club before I hit the exit.

Pulling out my phone, I noticed that I had a missed call so I hit REDIAL. The phone rung 3 times

and then there was a sexy voice that picked up saying "Get here daddy. I need to feel you inside of my walls. Get here!" Without any other words being said, we both disconnected with smiles on our faces. Smiling all the way to the club's entrance where the shorty from earlier stood waiting for some acknowledgment from me. I gave her the attention that she was looking for by telling her to hit me up when she was ready to finish what we started, she smiled and blew me a kiss in the air.

Walking out the door of the club and then having a moment. I have been having a lot of these moments lately. I was having a meltdown. Where did I park? Everything was a blur again. I couldn't remember which part of the city I was in. Where was I at? "Think Zavier think." I was beginning to talk to myself. I really couldn't remember. Panicking, then I started to walk up and down the street trying to look for my whip. Nothing was looking familiar to me, I didn't see Pepsi blue anywhere. I pulled out my phone, but who was I gonna call? Nobody knew where I was. Closing my eyes trying to see if things would get clearer in my mind. There was nothing, I just stood there. I was a big grown ass, strong ass man but I was in the middle of a mental breakdown. Everything that the doctors were trying to tell me were really becoming reality right before my very eyes. I was fucking losing it. I was losing my mind, literally. This is some scary ass shit and it saddens me

because we take so much in the world for granted including our minds and memory. This shit can't be happening to me. Not right now. I stood in one spot and turned in circles for clues. Nothing was clicking. People walked past me and looked as if I was crazy. That's what it felt like, I was going crazy. Some faces looked familiar and some didn't but they all knew me. This shit is scary as fuck man, I said in a tone loud enough to be heard by those close enough to me.

Standing on the sidewalk in the middle of nowhere it felt like. I looked and felt slow. Cars passed me by and honked their horns and I waved as if I knew what was going on. Pulling up to the sidewalk right next to me was a now-a-lata green Camaro. I had to check out my surroundings because you never knew who was who and what was what. Although in the situation that I was in I couldn't recognize much. Hopping out of the car was a tall guy walking towards me and it didn't click until he said "You good pop's?"

"Ramone?"? He shook his head for confirmation and then he tells me, "Dukes is looking for you and she told me that this was going to happen."

I looked at him with confusion and sadness in my eyes and told him how as soon as I walked out of the party. I lost everything. I can't remember where I

am. Where my car is? I'm just all fucked up son. Please promise me one thing Mone."

"What's that pops?" he said in a concerned tone.

He waited patiently until I got my thoughts together to focus on what I wanted to tell him. "Son, please look after your mother, dukes, the gym and please don't give up on your dreams. Go to the doctor on a regular and make sure that they constantly are doing brain exams on you so that you don't have to go through what I'm going through.

Ramone pulled up his where's my car app on his phone while Kenya waited patiently in the car as we got it together. "I found your car pop's you parked in the Middle Street Parking garage. So that's straight ahead." Ramone said pointing in the direction of the garage sign.

After walking straight ahead and into the garage beside Ramone while Kenya followed in the car is when I saw my Pepsi blue sitting right there on the ground level floor looking clean as a whistle. I knew the drill. I knew that Ramone wouldn't let me drive myself home. I got in the passenger and he drove while Kenya followed.

The 20 minute ride turned into what seemed like an hour ride back to my city. I listened as Ramone told me that he was beginning to be scared because my spells were coming a little more frequent now. It hurt me to know that my condition was bothering and scaring others. I had enough stress for the both of us and didn't need for him to stress as well.

I patted Ramone on the back as soon as he parked the car in the driveway and I thanked him for being the son that I never had. I thanked him for loving me unconditionally. We both teared up and shared a few sentimental words and moments until I yawned. Then I made my way out of the car and he made sure that I got into the house and then he left.

As soon as I stepped foot in the door I could smell what smelled like Armani. It was her favorite scent and I loved it. Following the scent and the trail of roses took me into my destination. I had to find my Armani. It was my baby, I could smell her. I wanted to taste her on my lips and feel her on the tip of my dick. I missed her so much, I couldn't understand why she was hiding from me. Why wouldn't she reveal herself? Didn't she miss me too?

Stepping into the bedroom is where I saw her fresh thongs lying on the bed along with her red teddy and her 5 inch stilettos. She was preparing for something, or maybe she just wanted to make her

man happy. While standing there thinking of how my night would surely end. I could hear what sounded like footsteps but I didn't see anyone. That's when I saw the curtains move in a flowing motion on their own. Jumping and looking around the room to see if I had missed something, but there was no one there but me. I didn't see anyone but something didn't seem right. Looking in the private bathroom was freaky as well. There was no signs of anyone in there but the tub was filled with hot water and the bubbles separated as if someone had just gotten in there. No signs of Raven anywhere. The water continued to move without a body. That was when I heard the alarm system start to talk letting me know that someone had just entered the house.

Another minute later I seen Raven sprinting up the stairs with a grin on her face. As if we didn't already know that Armani was no longer alive. It seemed as if we both were awaiting her return.

Raven smiled at me and said "Hey babe, where is she?" She must have smelled the same thing that I had just smelled. With anxiousness in her voice because I wasn't answering fast enough she shouted "Where is she Zavier?" She walked through the whole upstairs looking for Armani. I was speechless. Then once she walked into the private bathroom, she gasped for air and opened her eyes wide as if she had just seen a ghost. Or did she?

She stopped dead in her tracks and kept her head in the direction of the bath tub like she was seeing the same thing that I had just witnessed a little before her. Watching her look in the same direction was like watching a movie. The water was moving and it was looking like someone was making waves in the water. Raven grinned a seductive grin like someone had been inviting her to come in. Before I knew it Raven started to undress herself and was smiling while looking towards the water. She hopped in and looked as if she was enjoying the company of someone else. She looked up at me, it looked as if she wanted to say something. Before she spoke she turned back as if someone was saying something back to her. She then looked back at me once again and says "Come and get in with us baby." She giggled and watched as the water waved up and separated once again. It moved as if someone was getting out of the water now. She turned again to my direction and laughed a loud laugh. Something was definitely spooky going on. It felt as if I could feel my zipper slowly coming down. As I looked down, I saw nothing but felt the presence of someone and it was tripping me out. Looking towards Raven, her face was looking as if she was getting turned on.

It was her. I could tell because no one licked on me the way that she used to. She would always lick me from my belly button in a circling gesture to my thighs and then she would get to the head of my

122

manhood and then make a slurping sound as she teased from the head all the way to the shaft. Not a soul has ever compared to her dick sucking skills. That's exactly what they were. She had an amazing set of skills. She knew exactly what to do to get my undivided attention. She definitely had that. How was this possible? How was she here with us when she had gone on to another life without us? I was confused but now was not the time for the reservations.

I watched as Raven pleasured herself while she observed our interactions with one another. It was like we were all back together again. I could feel her leading me towards Raven and without me doing a thing I could feel my items of clothing start to slowly fall off. Was I dreaming or was this really happening.

"Well if I'm dreaming then I don't wanna wake up." I said aloud.

Raven comes back and says "Oh baby, trust me I promise you I won't wake you up."

Entering in the water was the three of us. There was Raven rubbing my back and licking my earlobe and then there was Armani straddling my lap. She sat there proudly, butt bald naked with my dick threatening to enter into her pussy. All of a sudden I could see her frame where at first I

could only feel her. She was simply beautiful. She had a glow about her and her smile was one of an angel. I had to taste her tongue, she was looking so damn good to me. It made me miss her even more than ever now. My Angel was here, back and better than ever. I went for her lips and she met me half way and like before Raven wanted in. She was having one of her jealous moments. The three of us swapped tongues together and everybody's hands were everywhere on everybody. I never want for this moment to end, but I knew that had to be too good to be true.

Armani squirmed and moved until she got what she wanted. My erect dick inside of her tight and wet pussy was what she was after and she got just that. As soon as I slide in her she slightly lifted up and whispered in my ear "Didn't I tell you that I didn't want you trying to replace me. I know that you were out looking and hoping to find another me. There will never be another me so stop searching and learn to simply love Raven. Men always want to love and fuck a million different women when the key is to simply find a million ways to love and fuck that one loyal woman. As soon as she said that she kissed me and then everything faded, there was no more Armani. I was there left in the tub with Raven and she was in my lap, not Armani. I looked around puzzled and off course, I knew for sure that what I was seeing and feeling before was real but it just all faded away.

Raven was fucking me for dear life and I was there zoned out and thinking of another woman. You might as well say that she was sexing herself and I was just there. I started to feel ashamed of myself. I had a devoted and loving wife that only wanted me and there I was longing for another.

Right then and there I felt a spark, a bit of passion came over me for Raven that I hadn't ever felt before. I fell in love with her all over again and this time it was stronger than ever. While Raven rode my dick I kissed her all over her upper body. She had passion marks tattooed all over her body. I kissed her passionately and ran my fingers through her hair as she changed gears on the stick shift. Pulling her down on my dick by her shoulders made her explode all on my dick. Her cum was warm and even with being in the water it still felt like heaven. I flipped her over and had her on her knees like a dog with her hands on the side of the tub. One of the requirements that I gave them when building this home was that the bathtub be unique and bigger than the average size bathtub. It was taller than the average tub and it looked like a miniature swimming pool. While watching her beg for more from behind her made me want to give her all of my dick right then and there. I wasn't ready for that just yet but by watching her it made it impossible not to enter her right then and there. I could feel her pussy lips pulsate on my dick and then she started to speak Spanish to me saying "**joderme papa' ma's**

duro," meaning fuck me harder daddy. That shit made me punish her pussy for a good 15 more strokes and then I burst all inside of her canal of greatness. "Shit! Fuck! Damn! I love you Ray for real! The rest of the night was spent loving on one another, like it was a new love affair.

Chapter 9
'Til Death Do Us Part

Loving Raven and Raven only from that point on was becoming natural for me now. I'm just upset that it took so many years of me not valuing her for me to get it. I got a winner and I've always known it but I took her for granted. I'm just glad that I was smart enough to make her my wife and she never decided to leave me. I'm a pretty lucky man to have a rider like her on my team, she had ridden with me through my bullshit. I can honestly say that she has been taking her vows seriously. She meant that she was going to stick by me, "until death do us part!"

Lately my condition has been getting a lot worse. I've been having constant headaches as well. I've just been trying to deal with them the best way I know how and not complain. God has blessed me way too much for me to complain about anything in this world. I've slowed down with going to these doctors. I'm just going to let God work on me and if it's meant then he will get me through it all.

Ramone is still doing his thing in the boxing world and becoming a household name. Anytime that he had anything going on career wise I was right

there to support him. Press conferences, fights, charity boxing events just anything that he had going on, I was his support. He acknowledged me as his Pops anytime someone asked him who he owed his success to. It was an honor to have worked and trained with him and watched him grow into the man that he is today. He's doing right by Kenya and they are now expecting their first child and he's talking about marrying her. He has really made me proud, he's doing the right things in his life.

Other than my health issues life has been like living a dream. For once in my life since my boxing days, I was really living life. I was really starting to enjoy the fruits of my labor. Raven has been the happiest that I have ever seen her in all of our years. I love to see her happy because if anybody deserves to be happy, it's her! We started to travel to more and began doing everything together. She even started to spend more time inside of the gym with me. She would bring her work there and work out of her issue inside of the gym. There was lunch dates daily and we also planned a lot of date nights with other couples. Life was great!

Chapter 10
Raven's Story Be A Love Slave No More

Reading my husband's last entry brought tears to my eyes and pain to my heart! It was really real, and I didn't want to accept what I knew to be reality…

Dear little black book….

With knowing and coming to grips with the fact that my last days may be quickly approaching. I want you to ALWAYS know that My soul may die but the love for you that I carry in my spirit will FOREVER live on.

Raven,

Even after my days here on earth have expired, I will still live within you for our love has no expiration date. When the cool wind breezes past you, I will be sure to steal a kiss and leave my mark all over your sweet and succulent lips. You will still feel my embrace at night, as I watch over your perfectly created soul. You were

designed in perfection specifically for me. I will be sure to thank the man upstairs for the amazing gift that he has blessed me with. Every chance that is given to me, I will drop in simply to nibble on your thighs and kiss all of the hiding places that have been placed between them. Rubbing your back after a long day and still massaging your feet will be my way of showing you my appreciation even after I am gone away. You're a queen and you deserve to forever be treated as such, so this will be my promise to you. I will forever assure that you will forever be on a pedestal. Even if I have to come back to you in a different form to make sure that your beauty forever shines through. I will make that my objective. When the cloud releases the raindrops and they fall upon your frame, just know that is me touching your soul to feel you with all of me. I may be gone in the physical but I will never leave you alone in the spiritual and that will forever be my promise to you. As long as you continue to allow me to make love to your mind and put your body at ease, I will continue to take care of all of your doubts and your fears.

(Even after I'm gone, that will be my mission)
I'm promising you my happily ever after, even after my after is no more. Just trust me, it's

possible baby girl. I will have everything worked out and God will not see me without you. I will dry each of your tears and make sure that you will not have to experience any sad or hard days alone. This is my dedication and my promise to you. I will forever and a day continue to love you even when you think that the love can no longer go on. I'm not concerned about you moving on and replacing me because I am confident that our yesterday's were just the beginning to our forevers! Thank you for forever being my 'Slave of Love' and for making every day of my life a memorable one. Even the days that I thought that I couldn't or didn't want to move on, you pushed me and made me see the beauty of it even through my sadness and pain. I love you Raven Wright and please share forever even after my final and last days with me!

Love Always, Speedy

This is Raven Wright and with tears in my eye's but joy in my heart, I will be finishing off my husband's story. Unfortunately he fought a good fight but like the Joe Tobias fight, the fight at life won the last battle. Because of Zavier's unwillingness to continue to go and get his exams and take the necessary medicines that they gave him to help out in his condition, his case worsened. His headaches

became unbearable and he was at a point where he was just miserable. Just when life had gotten better in some aspects, they had gotten worse in his health's view. I felt so sorry for him and wanted to take his pain away from him but unfortunately God didn't work like that. Zavier always felt as if he was being punished for all the wrongdoings that he has done throughout the years.

In reality he wasn't a bad husband and a lot of you may not agree with me but I have my reasons for thinking so. I will reveal a lot my reasoning for these thoughts once I drop my "In Memory Of" novel that I have been working on since the doctors diagnosed him with his chronic brain injury. Zavier "Speedy" Wright was a trooper and he definitely deserved to be recognized. I was hoping that he would have made it long enough to read his life's story. He would have been proud of my project that I have put together in his legacy. Zavier was my savior, where he thought that he had put me through so much, I like to think differently. The reason why I say that he saved me was because he actually did. There was no other way around it. My family was poor and had nothing but issues to offer me! He had dreams and he wasn't afraid of living them. He believed in himself, if no one else ever did. He showed me how it felt to receive real love. If not one soul loved me, Zavier Wright loved me.

My life wasn't the easiest for me, my younger years were hard to deal with. The average person couldn't deal with the walk that I had to walk. My shoes could never be walked in or filled. Unfortunately, I had to deal with a shit load of unfortunates but those same unfortunates made me the strong ride or die woman that I am today. The things that my parents put me through were things that were meant to break me, but God had other plans over my life!

My mother was the neighborhood functional crackhead and my father was a known child molester. My parents were a bad example for any and everyone. They were just taking up space on this earth. People hated when I said these things about my creators, but only I knew of the things that went on in our home. They had been rumors of my father molesting a few young ladies back in the day. I don't know all of the details because that was a hush hush situation and forbidden to be talked about. Even with knowing my father's ill ways and his bad reputation, my mother still didn't protect her only born child. Instead my mother allowed my father to molest me over the years as if it was right. Me being young and naive, I always thought that the things that my father did couldn't be wrong because my father would never do anything to hurt his own child, so I thought. I hated being there. I often had thoughts of death, running away from home and even killing the two of them. I felt that anywhere was better than being there with them. I wanted the Lord to rid me of them. I was

better off without them in my life. My mother was the sorriest woman in my eyes. How can you allow anyone to hurt your only baby girl? That was the question that I have asked myself for so many years.

I still remember one of the worst days of my childhood. It was a rainy Saturday morning and my mom had just came in from a 2 day drug vacation and she needed more money. She came in with one of her guy crack dealers and she watched as he eyed me as if I were a piece of meat. My father wasn't home at the time. He didn't play with my mother bringing her drug infested friends there where we laid our heads. I could tell when she walked in that she was high. That was not something that a 12 year old girl should have known anything about. She barged into my room all loud and indignant asking if I had any money or jewelry. As she asked me about money, her side kick looked around my room as well. He searched like he was looking for something in particular. They made me feel uneasy. I should never have to feel like this around my own mother. The sly faced man looked me over from head to toe and then came really close to me and seemed to smell my hair and then my neck. I felt creepy as hell. I couldn't believe my own mother wouldn't protect her own child. Just as the man began to run his fingers through my hair, I jerked away from him and shouted for him to get off of me. Just as I shouted, my daddy popped up around the corner. The look on my father's

face meant pure death. I was scared for the man. He didn't know what my mom had just gotten him into. My daddy saw red and I knew his look all too well. He went charging at the man and he proceeded to choke the life out of him, literally. My mother began to cry and shouted for my father to stop. She saved that man's life but wasn't expecting my father to turn the frustration back around onto her. He slapped my mother so hard that her face turnt. He started to yell all kinds of extremities at her like: "You fucking crackhead bitch! You let this lame ass mutha fucka put his filthy fuckin hands on my daughter, only I can do that!" He smacked her and then choked her as well. He tried to take her life. The man that my mom was with ran off and called the police while he was fuckin my momma up.

Long story short, once the police got there both of my parents were taken away from me. Just earlier that day my dad had just violated my body like he had done for so many times before. He would make me brush my hair and put on lipstick and makeup to get sexy for him. And then after that he would have his way with me. It was if I would take the place of my mother. My father was sick and really had a problem. I knew that he needed help. If you could do these things to your own flesh and blood, you simply had a problem. I hated my parents with everything in me. My daddy treated me more like his girlfriend then he did his daughter. No one was there to protect me, if I

were to try to fight him off of me then he would fight on me. The drug dealing man that my mother brought to the house ran off and called the police in fear of my father trying to kill my mother. When the cops had gotten there, I was balled up in a corner crying just thinking about how hard and unfortunate my life had become. It just wasn't fair that a child that didn't ask to come here, had to endure so much pain and wrongful doings.

My dad was in the room cleaning off his pistol. I'm assuming that he was going to do something to my mother or go and look for the drug supplier that ran his fingers through my hair. As soon as he loaded more bullets into the gun, there was a knock on the door. My mother was still lying on the floor sobbing while holding her face. She was so dramatic with it that it wasn't even funny. We paid my mother and her drama no mind because whenever she couldn't get her way, she acted out like she was the child. As soon as they saw the pistol in my father's hand, they drew their guns and read him his rights. They searched the house and that's when they saw my mother lying in the middle of the floor dramatically acting out. A female officer came over to me and asked me was I ok. Then asked me what happened. I didn't care what happened to either of them because they didn't give a damn about me or my wellbeing. Lying balled up in the corner, the female officer sat in the middle of the floor Indian-style to talk to me and I told her

everything. Not thinking of what would happen afterwards, I just spilled all the beans. I felt as if a weight had just been lifted off of my shoulders. It was time that it got out. Someone needed to know because I didn't deserve any of this. Everyone else let the things that they did slide by overlooking them, but not me. The curse had to be broken. They had to get what they deserved and I didn't even feel bad about what I had just done to them. My mother looked at me with sadness in her eyes, like I was supposed to feel an ounce of remorse for her. My father looked and me and called me all kinds of ungrateful and lying ass little bitches. I smiled because I knew that he was about to get what he deserved. They hauled both of my parents away but what I didn't think about was where I would go.

Little did I know but I went into foster care and that was just as worse. I was put with a family that didn't give a damn about me. They just wanted the check that came along with me. I wore hand me downs and I tried my best to make my hair look presentable. I have always been a pretty young lady, but my personality even after my hard life was what made me even more beautiful. I knew that when my time came that I would do the opposite that my parents had done with their lives. I knew that I wanted be the perfect mother to my child, if I ever had any. I also would be the perfect mate for my significant other and most importantly I would respect myself enough

137

to love me more than anything in life. I knew that it was gonna take the right man to notice me and my potential and that right guy just happened to be my angel here on earth, Zavier "Speedy Wright." He came along just as I thought that I had no one in my corner. He saw my imperfections and he then loved me that much more because of them.

Zavier used to live 3 doors down from the new house of my foster parents. He used to see how they did me and he felt sorry for me. We then formed a friendship and he was my shoulder to cry on and my ear to listen to me when I needed to talk. He didn't judge me, he only wanted better for me. He always told me that he would get me out of here and that he did. He grinded so hard in that gym so that he could stand true to his promise. He did just that, like the young folks say "He got me out the hood." It was plenty of nights where he fed me, wiped my tears, bought my tampons with the help from his mother. I owed him my life. No one knew me like he did and vice versa with myself. When I took my vows I took them seriously. I meant for better or for worse. I was proud to be my husband's love slave, but I would never submit to another man like I did my husband. No other man was worthy of my all like Zavier had proven to be.

Dear little black book...
(Moment of truth)
Raven's Edition

This journal entry will be the last and final entry for this journal before it gets published on my husband's behalf. I know that his story will inspire the life of others, because all that he ever wanted of others was for them to "Keep Fighting."

People often wondered how I stood behind my husband with reading the things that he shared in his journal entries. So to clear a few things up, my husband was a faithful husband! He developed the chronic brain damage and lost a lot of his brain functions. Then I later found out that he was diagnosed as a schizophrenic. The doctors broke the meaning of the word in the simplest terms as simply "Mr. Wright has a chronic mental disorder in which people interpret reality abnormally. They have a difficulty distinguishing between what's real and what is imaginary. Because of his CTE disorder, it caused an imbalance in the brain's chemistry." This explained a lot about some of the things that Zavier thought were going on in his world.

See I'm going to let y'all in on a little secret...

Speedy had several different women that he labeled his "Love Slave's."

There was:

Asia Monroe- His bare breasted love slave

Joy- The mistress from the gym

Santana Renee- The Christian "head doctor"

Naughty Nurse- His naughty night nurse from the hospital

Armani Bridges- Our other lover that he met in Vegas

Bridget- Door hostess from the club

Where people thought that my husband had several mistresses on me, they were wrong! It was my job as his wife to give him things to remember and to make his life worth loving while he was living. So each of these scandalous women were me. Raven Wright! I role played with my husband to keep our marriage spicy. I gave him things to look forward to and sex after his love for boxing was taken from him had become his escape from the sadness. So, yes I played the

part for my man. I was his whore, his slut, his bitch and also his angelic church girl. Now Armani Bridges was a different case, that's where his schizo came in to play. He had this whole imaginary relationship with this young lady and I going on in his damaged mind. The doctors warned me about these types of cases, once I told them that he was saying that he had another mate. He was secretly in love with this make believe, perfect and best of both worlds relationship that was going on in his head. He would hold whole conversations with me about this woman that was taking my place in my husband's head and also in his heart. Even though I knew of his condition and saw all of the warning signs that the doctors warned me about, I still would get jealous of this perfection of a fictitious woman. Even after he killed her off inside of his head he still would have visions and dreams of her. I knew that his condition was worsening when she had come back from his death of her. He visioned making love to her when he was there making love to me. He would call me her name and everything. But me being the loyal wife and supporter that he needed in his life, I played my positions. Whatever kind of woman he envisioned on having I was her. Whether he wanted sex in the car, on the elevator, in the shopping mall or in his own personal gym, I made

that happen! I held my promise to him. I promised him that I would forever give him several nights of continued excitement. I did that! I had fun doing it too. My husband was trained to go, if I wanted it several times a day, I got it several times a day from him. Whatever he wanted, my king got! He was living every man's dreams. He had a faithful wife, a faithful mistress, had sex with any woman that he wanted without hearing a nagging wife to fuss about any of it. I did my duties of being his 'Love Slave' up until the day that he took his last breath.

2 days before his 35th birthday, he said that he wanted to take Ramone and Kenya out to dinner and a movie. He just wanted to spend some time with them before he went away. I asked him what he meant by the last statement, "Before he went away." He wouldn't elaborate on it any further. I think that he was trying to tell me something. He knew that he was about to depart this earth. He wanted us all dressed up and ready to take over the world, as he would call it. We all wore the colors black and red and he also did something this day that he has never liked doing. He made sure that we took plenty of pictures. He smiled and posed and just seemed to be enjoying life. Although he had fun, it was something about the flash on the cameras that gave him a very

intense pain in his head. He often would get headaches but he said that this one felt different. The pain that he was feeling was from the aneurysm that he had developed in his brain. He had a blood-filled dilation of a blood vessel caused by a weakening of the vessel's wall. One of the biggest dangers with his aneurysm was that when some of the blood flowing through his artery diverted into the aneurysm sac. While on the car ride home after Ramone was taking us home all of a sudden there was a loss of consciousness from Zavier. His headache had gotten worse and that was when the sac ruptured. That lead to his head to start hemorrhaging. There was no bringing him back from that. It killed him instantly and we didn't even realize that we had lost him so sudden.

Ramone took it so hard because Zavier was his only father figure since his father had died. He went into a shell and seemed as if he didn't wanna do his boxing anymore. Kenya and I had to be strong for him because he was losing it right before our eyes.

Right before Zavier's home-going service, the pastor put some holy water on Ramone's head and began to say a brief prayer. The prayer helped with Ramone's nerves because he was now relaxed and thinking of the good times that they

shared. As Ramone walked up to the casket, he kissed Zavier on the forehead and whispered the words "I love you pops and I promise I will make you so proud of me. Your legacy will continue to live on through me!" When I read Ramone's lips it brought tears to my eye's with knowing even though I was unable to give my husband a baby, we were still blessed with a child! Ramone's mother sat right by my side at the funeral, just as I did her at her husband's funeral. They stayed by my side as I needed them too and it made me realize how blessed that I was.

I missed my husband dearly but I knew that God needed him more than I did. His time here on earth had expired, for the Lord only was loaning him to us just temporarily! It was time that the Lord needed him to do work in his permanent home, through the pearly gates. I easily wanted to be selfish and get mad with God about taking my husband away but I had to pray on it. I then realized that I had to respect the fact that it was his time to go. I have a lifetime of memories and pictures to keep me grounded, but I will never stop missing or loving my husband until the day that I join him. I was his very own personal love slave and there was nothing that I wouldn't do for Zavier because he would do the same for me! (Until next time)...

Releasing my special project "In Memory Of Zavier Speedy" Wright" story exactly a month after his passing was hard but it was also a joyous occasion as well. I wanted the world to see life through the one that truly knew my husband, myself. I had to let the world know how he saved my life and how I was a love slave for my man. He deserved every piece of pussy that he got from me and if he said that he wanted to experience fucking a gang of California sluts then his California sluts I would have been. I would have been a gang of slutty dressing, dick sucking and submissive whores that he wished for. I was into pleasing my man and that was what I was put on this earth to do!

-Love Slave No More-

There it was time for me to go onto the Lion News morning show where I would read my final passage from my novel that I was releasing. I was needing to give myself closure and to prepare for my healing process to begin. My soul was cleansing and I was finding peace within myself again. I felt kind of lost because I no longer had Zavier here to validate me and my feelings over my life. He was my everything. He was the positive force that I needed in my life to make it through the rough times in any situation.

So in memory of my fighter that fought that good fight, I hope that this passage finds you remembering our happy times and all of the great sex that we shared amongst you and my many alter ego's that I have blessed you with over the years.

Until we meet again Mr. Zavier Wright.

Rest Easy my king and watch as our novel makes it to the top! This one's for you Speedy!

My declaration of LOVE!

Anitra Hill is a native of Hampton, VA. Writing is her passion and her therapy that she wishes to share with the world. She has a writing goal of giving her readers a much needed escape from everyday reality.

With the huge success of "The Right One At The Wrong Time," Anitra followed up with "Love Slave."

Anitra continues to stay busy writing and traveling sharing her work with all of her readers.